"I gave my word that I would protect you. I'm honor bound to do that."

"Your honor doesn't require that you die for me." Amelia reined in her horse. When Harad moved up beside her, she reached out, urging him to stop. "I don't expect you to spend the rest of your life protecting me."

She was so sincere and brave that Harad couldn't resist. "What if that's the way I choose to spend my time?" he asked.

Amelia looked directly into his eyes. "I'd say you were a man who enjoyed thankless tasks," she answered.

Harad's laughter was long and loud. "A glutton for punishment is the phrase I've heard." He leaned over and brushed his lips to hers. "Call me a fool, but nothing will prevent me from protecting you. Not even your own hardheadedness."

Dear Harlequin Intrigue Reader,

Summer lovin' holds not only passion, but also danger! Splash into a whirlpool of suspense with these four new titles!

Return to the desert sands of Egypt with your favorite black cat in *Familiar Oasis*, the companion title in Caroline Burnes's FEAR FAMILIAR: DESERT MYSTERIES miniseries. This time Familiar must help high-powered executive Amelia Corbet, who stumbles on an evil plot when trying to save her sister. But who will save Amelia from the dark and brooding desert dweller who is intent on capturing her for his own?

Ann Voss Peterson brings you the second installment in our powerhouse CHICAGO CONFIDENTIAL continuity. Law Davies is not only an attorney, but an undercover agent determined to rescue his one and only love from a dangerous cult—and he is *Laying Down the Law*.

Travel with bestselling author Joanna Wayne to the American South as she continues her ongoing series HIDDEN PASSIONS. In *Mystic Isle*, Kathryn Morland must trust a sexy and seemingly dangerous stranger—who is actually an undercover ex-cop!—to help her escape from the Louisiana bayou alive!

And we are so pleased to present you with a story from newcomer Kasi Blake that is as big as Texas itself! Two years widowed, Julia Keller is confronted on her Texas ranch by a lone lawman with the face of her dead beloved husband. Is he really her long-lost mate and father of her child—or an impostor? That is the question for this *Would-Be Wife*.

Enjoy all four!

Denise O'Sullivan
Associate Senior Editor
Harlequin Intrigue

FAMILIAR OASIS

CAROLINE BURNES

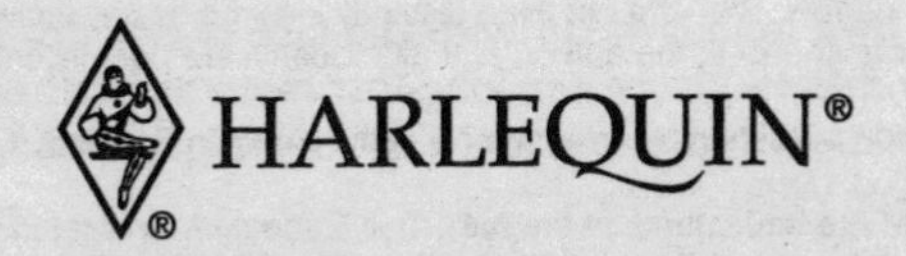

TORONTO • NEW YORK • LONDON
AMSTERDAM • PARIS • SYDNEY • HAMBURG
STOCKHOLM • ATHENS • TOKYO • MILAN • MADRID
PRAGUE • WARSAW • BUDAPEST • AUCKLAND

ISBN 0-373-22673-X

FAMILIAR OASIS

This edition published by arrangement with Harlequin Books S.A.

Visit us at www.eHarlequin.com

Printed in U.S.A.

ABOUT THE AUTHOR

Caroline Burnes continues her life as doorman and can opener for her six cats and three dogs. E. A. Poe, the prototype cat for Familiar, rules as king of the ranch, followed by his lieutenants, Miss Vesta, Gumbo, Chester, Maggie the Cat and Ash. The dogs, though a more lowly life form, are tolerated as foot soldiers by the cats. They are Sweetie Pie, Maybelline and Corky.

Books by Caroline Burnes

HARLEQUIN INTRIGUE

86—A DEADLY BREED
100—MEASURE OF DECEIT
115—PHANTOM FILLY
134—FEAR FAMILIAR*
154—THE JAGUAR'S EYE
186—DEADLY CURRENTS
204—FATAL INGREDIENTS
215—TOO FAMILIAR*
229—HOODWINKED
241—FLESH AND BLOOD
256—THRICE FAMILIAR*
267—CUTTING EDGE
277—SHADES OF FAMILIAR*
293—FAMILIAR REMEDY*
322—FAMILIAR TALE*
343—BEWITCHING FAMILIAR*
399—A CHRISTMAS KISS
409—MIDNIGHT PREY
426—FAMILIAR HEART*
452—FAMILIAR FIRE*
485—REMEMBER ME, COWBOY
502—FAMILIAR VALENTINE*
525—AFTER DARK
"Familiar Stranger"*
542—FAMILIAR CHRISTMAS*
554—TEXAS MIDNIGHT
570—FAMILIAR OBSESSION*
614—FAMILIAR LULLABY*
635—MIDNIGHT BURNING
669—FAMILIAR MIRAGE*†
673—FAMILIAR OASIS*†

*Fear Familiar
†Fear Familiar: Desert Mysteries

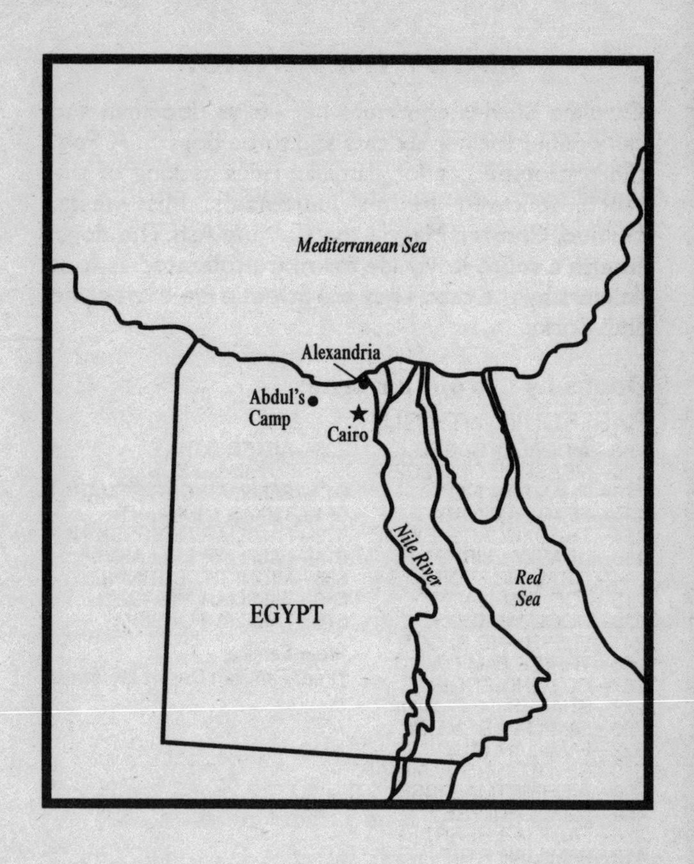
Mediterranean Sea
Alexandria
Abdul's Camp
Cairo
Nile River
Red Sea
EGYPT

CAST OF CHARACTERS

Familiar—After adventuring with Beth Bradshaw in the desert sands of Egypt, Familiar is ready for food, sleep and a return ticket to the U.S.A. until he finds himself swept up in an attack on Amelia Corbet, Beth's "adopted" sister.

Amelia Corbet—High-powered executive Amelia lands in Alexandria to rush to the aid of Beth Bradshaw. But Amelia becomes the intended victim of a foul plan only moments after she arrives.

Harad Dukhan—Harad gave up his desert heritage to pursue a career in the modern world, but his heart is still with the desert people of his mother. Amelia Corbet's arrival pulls Harad into an intrigue where not only his heart, but his life, is at stake.

Mauve Killigan—Perky and always on the spot when trouble threatens, Mauve might be part of the solution or part of the problem.

Dr. Kaffar Mosheen—Handsome and talented in the use of poisons, Kaffar is either a lifesaver or an "attempted" murderer.

Abdul—Leader of a maurading nomadic band that is best described as pirates of the sand, Abdul is a self-proclaimed thief. But is he a trader in flesh?

Marie Johnson—Harad's secretary knows all of his secrets, as well as his whereabouts at all times. Is she spilling the beans to his enemies?

Nazar Bettina—He escaped capture and has vanished from Egypt. Is he really gone?

Keya—Harad offered her banishment instead of prison. Was it a wise choice or a deadly mistake?

To my brother and sister-in-law, David and Gail.
They've rescued, spayed and neutered, and loved and buried dozens of felines. When others turned their backs on unwanted animals, they opened their home.

Chapter One

The heat of Alexandria is intense, but after my little sojourn in the desert, I vowed not to complain about minor things anymore. All I can say is that if I never have to ride on a horse again for the rest of my life, it'll be too soon.

Peter and Eleanor, my humanoids, have finished the veterinarian symposium for which they came to this sunburnt metropolis, and they've given me fair warning that they're leaving in four days. For the moment, they want to sightsee and vacation a little. They've made it clear they want me back at our hotel each night by midnight. Can you believe they're actually trying to set a curfew for me, Familiar, black cat detective? Right. That only goes to show how deluded humanoids can be. Cats do not believe in curfews. Nor are we willingly ordered about for any reason.

But I forgive my humans. They've been worried about me, and as I know from experience, it's tough to relax and have fun when you're worried about someone you love.

The truth is, a midnight curfew sounds sort of good. I'm worn out. All I really have left to do is to make sure Amelia Corbet arrives in Alexandria safely, and that Mauve meets her and tells her that Beth is safe and happily on her way to wedded bliss in the desert.

Beth wanted to wait for Amelia to arrive. She wanted her "sister" to be with her for the wedding. But the Moon of Con was only six days off, and she had to hustle to get to the lost city for the ceremony during the full moon. It was important to Omar, a tradition of his people for many centuries. So now it's up to Mauve to convince Amelia that all is well with Beth and that her "sister" had chosen wisely in marrying a desert sheik.

I would have adored seeing this mystical marriage ceremony, but someone had to come back to the city and tie up the loose ends. Besides, as I've mentioned, I have a small responsibility not to worry my humanoids more than is absolutely necessary. Beth and Omar are fine. It's time for me to put a little effort into Peter and Eleanor.

I can't help but wonder, though, if Beth will continue with her research. She's a talented archeologist and anthropologist, and her theory about the great Con was right on target.

She came to Egypt to prove that Con was one of the most powerful females in history, and she did that. The question is, will she publish her research and risk exposing Omar's protected heritage, or will she keep the secret?

I guess time will tell. For now, though, I see a big

Pan-Am bird circling the airport and heading for a landing strip. Amelia should be on this flight. So where is Mauve? I don't see a sign of the redhead. Curiouser and curiouser, as Alice would say. Mauve struck me as someone who would do what she said she'd do. She said she'd meet Amelia, explain the situation and make sure Amelia didn't spend a moment worrying. I suppose I'll have to figure out a way to detain Ms. Corbet until Mauve gets here.

The passengers are disembarking. Beth said Amelia is her exact opposite. Tall, blond vivacious and tough as nails. And there she is! Wow! She looks as if she walked right off a Paris runway. And I can just hear Nancy Sinatra in the background singing, "These boots are made for walking." Amelia Corbet acts as though she could walk over General Patton. Beth wasn't exaggerating when she said the woman she grew up with and considers her adopted sister is nothing like herself. Let me swagger on over and check out this babe up close.

AMELIA WAS TIRED, gritty, annoyed and sick with worry as she exited the plane and stepped into a gate area of the Alexandria airport. The hot Egyptian summer air smacked into her hard. She hated heat. She hated the sun. She hated the fear that made her stomach feel as if someone had punched her.

Beth wasn't the kind of person to send cryptic messages or play games. Her adopted sister was in real trouble.

Amelia pulled her suitcase behind her. Long ago

she'd learned to pack light and never check a bag. Customs was going to take long enough—she had no intention of wasting precious time in baggage claim. She had to find her sister and make certain Beth was okay, and then she had to get on to Paris.

The public relations/advertising firm where she was a senior vice president had just won the coveted French account of Momante, producer of the world's most sensual perfume. Amelia was personally handling the entire campaign. It was a plum of an assignment, and she'd scrapped hard to get it. Once Beth was safe, Amelia'd be on her way to a country that understood the finer things in life, such as perfume, chocolate, champagne and men who knew how to make a woman feel like a woman.

After her latest breakup—she'd known better than to let things with the *GQ* model get serious—she needed a man who was more intrigued by his woman's appearance than by his own. She chuckled softly to herself at the irony of her situation. Roberto, with his dark Latino charm and eyes that could summon a look of passion on cue, had been as much fun as an egomaniac could be. But it had ended badly, and Amelia had made a solemn vow not to let another man close to her heart.

Amelia's hand went to the necklace at her throat, her slender fingers catching the gold scarab. It had arrived by special courier only moments before she got in the cab to head to the airport. The urgent arrival of this package, so soon after the package full of strange photographs Beth had sent her, had increased

Amelia's fear for her sister. The note from Beth had asked her to wear the necklace prominently so that Amelia could be identified.

Identified by whom? First there was the packet from Beth with the disk, the photos and the word Merlin—their private childhood code for danger. Then she'd got another urgent message from Mauve Parker saying Beth was in danger.

And where, exactly, was Beth?

Stuffed in Amelia's suitcase were the strange photographs of what looked like some ancient and indecipherable language. It was a combination of scratches and pictures that gave Amelia a headache every time she studied it. She didn't have to strain her imagination to see Beth poring over the pictures, delight evident.

Beth had always been the one who preferred math equations, puzzles, measuring things and making them fit. Beth was the detail person, the perfectionist. Amelia was all action and no introspection.

And that was just the way she liked her life. Fast, busy and exciting.

She scanned the airport, halting so abruptly that a man walking behind her actually stumbled into her. She felt a sharp sting in the back of her neck as she regained her balance.

"I'm sorry," Amelia said, her hand still fingering the pendant she wore on her neck. The man's eyes locked on the medallion and then slid up her face. Her neck was burning.

"No need to apologize," he said in only slightly accented English. He brushed past her and was gone.

Amelia searched the airport, her blue gaze moving from one unfamiliar face to another. Everyone was bustling about as if they knew exactly where they were going. And there were cats everywhere! She frowned as she realized that cats were lounging on chairs, sleeping in the sun that shafted in through the windows, and trotting along the concourses. The felines had taken over the airport, and no one seemed to notice.

A large black cat began to rub on her leg. Amelia sidestepped. "Shoo!" she said. She didn't particularly like cats. They were arrogant and demanding. Nothing like her J.J., the Jack Russell and whippet mix that she'd rescued from the pound.

She started to walk forward, still a little puzzled as to why someone wasn't waiting for her. To her surprise, the cat snagged her black leather boots with a sharp claw.

"Hey!" she said, trying to shake free. When he wouldn't retract his claws, she looked around for help. Not a single person would even look in her direction.

"Release me," she said to the cat, aware that he was staring right into her eyes as if he had something to tell her.

"Ms. Corbet?"

The voice was low, dark and compelling. Amelia forgot the cat as she turned to confront the man who'd spoken to her.

"Yes, I'm Amelia Corbet. And you are?" She put out her hand. A wave of dizziness came out of nowhere and smacked into her. The hand she'd extended pressed against the handsome stranger's chest as she tried to block her fall. Her body was suddenly completely out of control. She tried to speak, but her throat had grown sluggish and thick. Her tongue couldn't move, and she could hear the quick, panicked breaths she was dragging into her lungs.

"Help me." She mouthed the words, aware that no sound had come from her mouth. Though she couldn't talk, she could see that the man holding her was aware that something was very wrong. His dark eyes filled with worry as he began shouting for help.

It was the last thing Amelia remembered.

HARAD DUKHAN HELD the woman in his arms as he waited for medical help. Amelia Corbet had been a total shock to him, as had the fact that Mauve was not in the airport to meet Beth's sister. He was there only because his brother Omar had asked him to make sure Amelia understood that Beth was happy. Her only regret was that her adopted family didn't have time to attend the ceremony because of the full moon.

It was with relief that Harad helped the paramedics place the tall, thin blonde on a stretcher and prepare her for transport to the hospital. She was out cold, Harad saw. Cold and pale, and yet her forehead was beaded with perspiration. He lifted one of her hands. It was lifeless and chilled. Only minutes before, she'd been striding across the airport concourse like the Queen of Sheba.

Harad had seen the incident where the man had stumbled into Amelia. Just as the paramedics lifted the stretcher, Harad decided to play a hunch. He halted them a moment and brushed back Amelia's hair. The first thing he saw was the golden scarab hanging from the expensive gold chain. It was a work of art, and very Egyptian. He moved it away and began to examine her skin. The mark on the right side of her neck was big, angry and red.

"Check her for some kind of nervous system drug," Harad said tersely to the medics. He showed them the spot. "I think she was poisoned." His gut instinct was to keep the woman away from his people and their secrets.

With the siren wailing, the ambulance pulled away from the airport, and Harad waited for airport security. He would have to make a statement before he left. To do otherwise would draw attention to himself, and right now, he didn't want any governmental scrutiny of Dukhan Enterprises.

"Omar, I'm going to kick your butt when I finally find you," Harad vowed, thinking of his younger brother. It was then he noticed the black cat. He had his own black feline, Tut. And there were thousands of black cats in Alexandria. This one was distinctive, though. It looked exactly like the cat that had been involved with his brother and the female anthropologist.

"Familiar?" He walked toward the feline. This

was the cat who'd saved his brother's fiancée, Beth Bradshaw. It was because of Omar and Beth that Harad now found himself in the middle of police scrutiny.

"Meow." The cat came toward him, black tail straight in the air, tip twitching. "Meow." Familiar's golden gaze was unblinking.

"My brother insists you are an extraordinary creature," Harad said, sighing. "I'm sure your presence here has something to do with Ms. Corbet."

"Meow."

Harad bent down to stroke the cat, when he heard his name called.

"Mr. Dukhan, would you come with us?"

Harad followed the two airport security guards through the concourse to the plush office where he would be given hot tea and a cigar, if he wished. To his amusement, he saw that the black cat was following right on his heels. Well, Familiar would be an interesting distraction.

AMELIA OPENED her eyes and then closed them again. Everything in the room seemed to spin around her, and she felt her stomach revolt against the sensation.

"Well, the patient has regained consciousness," an unfamiliar female voice said with a hint of excitement.

Opening one eye a slit, she finally focused on a redhead who was sitting in a chair beside the bed.

"Who are you?" Amelia asked. She had a vague memory of a very handsome man, dark and somehow foreboding. He'd held her in his arms. She could remember the extraordinary fabric of his suit, the smell of his cologne, the sense of some exotic danger.

"I'm Mauve, Beth's associate. Beth asked me to meet you in the airport, but as I was going inside, someone stole my purse. I ran after the man, but I lost him in the crowd. So, I was a little late. Looks like you had a welcoming committee of your own."

The words seemed to ping against Amelia's forehead, but she managed to grasp their meaning. "There was a man..."

"Harad Dukhan. The police are questioning him now," Mauve supplied. "He's a looker, isn't he?"

"What happened to me?" Amelia wasn't in the mood to discuss Harad's appearance. She was annoyed that she even remembered what he looked like. She'd sworn off men.

"Someone injected something into your neck. Didn't you feel a pinprick or another sharp sensation?" Mauve got up and leaned over Amelia. She brushed a hand over Amelia's neck. "Right there."

"Yes!" Amelia's fingers explored the spot where she'd earlier felt the stinging sensation just as a man had stumbled into her in the airport. It had been deliberate. "What did he inject me with?" she asked.

"Some type of plant poison. The doctor said the name, but plants aren't my area of expertise. At any rate, the antidote worked. He said you should be feeling better in an hour or so."

"And this Harad Dukhan. What about him?"

"Soon to be your brother-in-law," Mauve said

breezily. ‘‘If you prefer the desert type, which your sister obviously does, Omar’s the poster child for handsomest man of the year. I, personally, like that tailored, well-groomed, reeking-of-money-and-success aura that Harad projects. What about you?’’

‘‘There’s not a man breathing who could interest me right now,’’ Amelia said. She meant every word of it.

Mauve’s eyebrows arched. ‘‘That’s tempting fate, girl,’’ she said brightly. ‘‘If there’s one thing I’ve learned, it’s that fate always seems to throw exactly what we don’t want right into the middle of our path.’’

‘‘I want to see my sister,’’ Amelia said, suddenly overcome with worry. ‘‘Is she hurt or sick or in some kind of danger?’’

Mauve took Amelia’s hand and held it. ‘‘Beth *was* in a lot of trouble. Now your sister is safe and happy. Very happy. She’s going to marry Omar Dukhan.’’

‘‘What?’’ Amelia tried to push herself up in bed, but what felt like a sledgehammer slamming into her skull stopped her. Moaning, she gently let her head rest back on the pillow.

‘‘The doc said there would be some pain and dizziness,’’ Mauve told her. ‘‘He said it would go away in an hour or two. Any motion or bright light will set it off, though. He advised you to stay in bed and remain as still as possible. If you’re anything like Beth, though, I just wasted my breath.’’

‘‘I can’t move,’’ Amelia said between gritted teeth. ‘‘This man that Beth is marrying. What about him?

Beth hasn't been over here but a couple of weeks. How can she marry someone she's only known for fourteen days? What does he do? Where are they? Can you bring me to them?''

She stopped her assault of questions only when she heard Mauve softly laughing at her. ''What's so funny?''

''You and Beth are so different, yet you're so much alike. First let me say that Beth is doing exactly as she wants. She's head over heels in love. Omar, though at first he was deceptive, seems to be a man of honor. And he loves your sister very much.''

''That all *sounds* fine. What does this character do for a living?''

Mauve hesitated. ''That's sort of hard to say. He's a desert guide, and he has the most incredible Arabian stallion. I think he and his tribe...oh, yeah, he's some kind of ruler of this tribe of nomads, and—''

''Wait just one minute.'' Amelia kept her eyes shut tight as she tried not to move. ''He's a *nomad?*''

''Right,'' Mauve said, and this time there was the first hint of doubt in her voice. ''It's not exactly like it sounds, Amelia. He's very smart and well educated and—they're going to be fine now that the bad guys are in jail and the orbus plant, which Omar and Harad's family once used to predict the future, has been destroyed. Really, Beth was in danger when her co-workers and some financial backers were trying to use to her to get their hands on that plant.''

''Wait a minute!'' Amelia ground her teeth. ''Beth

was looking for a lost city. At least, that's what she said.''

''She was. The lost City of Con. Con was a female tribal ruler who had the gift of prophecy. It's an inherited trait in the Dukhan family. But this plant, the orbus, played a vital role in bringing the dreams on. Omar and Harad's mother, Aleta, saw that the plant would be dangerous if it fell into the wrong hands, so she destroyed it. So now Beth is safe and she'll live happily ever after with Omar. She wanted to hold the wedding until the Corbets could get here, but the full moon of July is the Moon of Con and the wedding had to take place then because of all the 'mystical stuff'.''

Amelia wondered if she was still dreaming. Nothing Mauve was saying sounded in the least like her practical sister. ''My sister is out in the desert somewhere living in a tent with a nomad chieftain and his orbus-taking family, surrounded by sand and camels, and you think it's okay?'' Amelia clipped her words as her head pounded.

''It's what Beth loves,'' Mauve said softly. ''You're different than she is, Amelia. You can't judge her choices by what you would want.''

''My sister is in line for the top museum job in the Southwest. She would have a staff of two dozen archeologists and anthropologists to help her preserve the Oconowasee Indians, a culture she's studied for the past ten years. She adores that people. She's wanted that job since she was twelve years old. You can't tell me that she'd rather ride across the desert on the back of a camel, playing harem girl to some sheik.''

''Amelia, I think—''

''As soon as I can get up from here, you're going to take me to Beth.''

''Of course,'' Mauve said, and there was a strange tone to her voice. ''I think you should know—''

''And once I get my hands on this desert Don Juan, he's going to rethink his kidnapping ways. My sister is an innocent in the ways of men, but I'm not. Heck, how many wives does this sheik have already?''

''My brother has not yet taken a wife. When he does, he will marry only one woman.'' The male voice was smooth, silky and edged with steel. ''Perhaps your sister would be better served if you left your cartoon ideas about my country behind you.''

Amelia knew that to open her eyes would bring pain, but she opened them nonetheless. The pounding started right behind her lids, and it wasn't helped at all by the hot flush of blood that suffused her cheeks. Her words had been rash and angry, and unfair.

''I didn't hear you come in,'' she said, staring at the man who'd helped her in the airport. She'd begun to believe that she might have imagined him, but there he stood, more than six feet tall, broad shoulders and slim hips, all encased in an Armani suit the color of desert sand. It did everything to show off his natural olive complexion and the glint of his dark brown eyes.

''I tried to give you a heads up,'' Mauve said

smugly, "but you wouldn't let me get a word in edgewise."

"Beth would tell you it's one of my worst character flaws," Amelia said. "I'm sorry." She continued to look at the handsome man, who felt no need to hide his irritation with her. "I owe you an apology also. And your brother. You're right, I don't know him."

Harad Dukhan nodded. A change shifted over his face, seemingly as if he willed his anger to dissipate. He stepped closer to the bed. "I've spoken with the doctor. You were deliberately poisoned, Ms. Corbet. The dose was probably not meant to be fatal. For some reason, someone wanted you immobilized in the airport. Can you think why that would be so?"

Amelia watched Harad Dukhan very closely as he spoke. He was trying hard to be casual, but there was a tension to the man that told her he felt otherwise. She wasn't a scientist, and she hadn't spent the last ten years studying ancient ruins, but she was a damn good judge of human nature, and Harad Dukhan was hiding something.

"I never carry cash or jewels. I brought one bag with a few clothes." She started to shake her head, but the motion made her head pound harder. "No one even knew I was coming here," she finally said. "I left without notifying anyone in my office. I'd hoped to see Beth, make sure she was okay and get on to Paris before anyone even noticed I'd dropped out of sight for a night."

"Someone noticed," Harad said.

"Is my sister safe?" Amelia asked.

Harad nodded. ''As safe as she can possibly be. My brother would give his life to protect her, and he's a fierce warrior when it comes to the people and things he loves.''

''I have to see her. As soon as possible,'' Amelia said.

''We can discuss it,'' Harad said, ''when you are fully recovered.''

Chapter Two

Harad wanted only to close his eyes, open them, and find that he was not in a hospital room with the blond, willful and very American Amelia Corbet. Though she was one of the most attractive women he'd ever seen—and he'd made it a point to see a lot of women—she was opinionated, bossy and without the first hint of manners. So many women, when they stepped into the business world, lost their femininity. Amelia Corbet would walk over a man and never even look back to see if her spiked heels had left holes in the body.

Because of his brother, Harad knew Amelia was his responsibility until he could get her out of Egypt and on her way to wherever it was that she did her jet-set business. Which would be as soon as possible. He did not trust her—especially with the secrets of his people.

"How long before the doctor will release you?" he asked, forcing his voice to a level of politeness.

Mauve jumped in with the answer. "The doctor said he would come by before dinner. If Amelia's health checks out, she can leave right after that,'' she said.

Harad glanced down at his wristwatch. Maybe half an hour, but it would be the next day before she could catch a flight out. ''I'll book a room for you in the Abbula Hotel,'' he offered. ''And for you, Mauve. I know you've been at the Crescent, but I'd like you to be near Amelia if you don't mind. The Abbula is a *comfortable* blend of my culture and your own, Ms. Corbet. Perhaps you won't feel so much that you've been dropped in the middle of barbarians.''

He saw the flush creep over her cheeks once again and felt a dart of shame at his own conduct. At least Amelia had the upbringing to be ashamed of herself. And she had apologized. Now he had been the one to show rudeness.

''That would be lovely, Mr. Dukhan,'' Amelia said with perfect grace. ''But it isn't necessary. I'm sure that I can manage in Alexandria as well as I can in any other *international* city.''

There was just enough challenge in her voice to make Harad smile. She was a woman of spirit, a trait he admired in both men and women. ''My offer was not meant to imply that you needed assistance, only that I would like to extend the courtesy. Your first impression of my country could not possibly be favorable. I assure you that most visitors aren't accosted in the airport. While you are here, I want you to see the best of what Alexandria has to offer.''

He could see that Amelia wasn't fooled one little bit, but she nodded and thanked him sweetly.

A tap at the door signaled the arrival of the doctor. Mauve greeted the white-coated gentleman like an old friend, and Harad remembered that the redhead had been poisoned, too. Someone had put something in her coffee and Dr. Rashad had taken care of her—with some help from Omar. In fact, Beth Bradshaw's entire quest to find the lost City of Con had been fraught with dangerous incidents. But Omar, Harad, Beth and the uncanny black feline, Familiar, had rounded up the men responsible for trying to injure Beth and to steal her research. Those men were behind bars.

So why had someone attacked Amelia? The question niggled in the back of his brain as he started to make his excuses and step from the room to allow the doctor time to examine Amelia.

Another tap at the door halted him. It swung wide to reveal a tall man with broad shoulders and a long stride who stepped immediately to Amelia's side. He carried a clipboard, and his dark eyes were solemn as they examined Amelia.

"Ms. Corbet, this is Dr. Mosheen." Dr. Rashad made the introductions. "He specializes in poisons."

"Kaffar Mosheen," the man said, stepping slightly in front of Harad as he took Amelia's hand. He kissed it in a smooth, continental gesture.

"Dr. Mosheen is a botanist as well as a doctor," Dr. Rashad explained. "He provided the antidote for you, and he's expressed a personal interest in your case. He asked to meet you. I hope you don't mind."

"Not at all," Amelia said, turning to the taller doctor. "Thank you, Dr. Mosheen. I was very sick, but I'm feeling much better now."

Harad felt his jaw muscles twitch at the way Amelia was smiling up into the doctor's eyes. She was looking at him as if he had descended from heaven.

"The poison was very interesting," Dr. Mosheen said. He leaned toward Amelia and unerringly bent to examine her neck. "The point of injection was fortunate. It missed the arteries. It is my guess that your assailant had a small ring that would spring open and reveal a tiny needle. The needle had been dipped in the poison, which is not normally lethal. My supposition is that the incident was intended to make you very sick and dizzy. You were spared much of the discomfort thanks to your friend, who acted so quickly and called an ambulance. My curiosity is aroused, though. It is a very old poison not commonly used against humans."

"You're making us feel better and better," Mauve said with a hint of sarcasm. "Next you'll tell us that the poison is the weapon of choice of either a satanic cult or a terrorist group bent on killing all Americans."

Dr. Mosheen laughed softly, but his eyes remained serious. "Not quite so dramatic. The poison comes from a common plant, therefore many people could have knowledge of its use. In a very diluted form it's used to spray cotton plants to kill insects." He shrugged. "It would not be difficult to find. An attack of this sort is not the style of a terrorist group. More likely the attacker was a common thief who targeted Ms. Corbet as a wealthy American traveler."

"I'm sure you've informed the police of all this," Harad cut in.

He saw Amelia's eyebrows lift slightly, and he knew his tone had been curt.

"Yes, the authorities are informed," Dr. Mosheen said smoothly. "They will want to question Ms. Corbet tomorrow, when she is completely recovered. I will send them to your hotel—"

"I'll make sure she gets to the police department," Harad said. "Can Ms. Corbet leave now?" He addressed the question to the older doctor.

"Yes," Dr. Rashad said. "She must be watched, though."

Kaffar Mosheen seemed oblivious to Harad's terse behavior. He turned back to Amelia. "If you are staying in Alexandria, I'd very much like to talk with you about the sensations of the drug—and that interesting pendant you're wearing." He reached into the pocket of his white coat and pulled out a business card and pressed it gently into Amelia's hand. "Please call me if you find you have a free hour. It would greatly help my research."

"Yes, thank you, Doctor." Amelia took the card.

Both doctors left the room, already talking about another case. Harad found himself standing at the door, feeling completely out of place. It wasn't an emotion he'd felt often, and he distinctly disliked it.

"If you'll excuse me," Amelia said, "I'll dress with Mauve's help."

Harad nodded and stepped outside the door without a word. He took up his position in the hallway, waiting for the women. Amelia was a burden transferred from his brother's back to his own. So why had he gotten so irritated at the way Dr. Mosheen had been coming on to her? And it had been a come-on. Research! Bah! The doctor recognized a beautiful woman when he saw one, and he was not so wrapped up in his *research* that he wasn't interested in making a move on the American.

AMELIA GRINNED as she looked into Mauve's dancing eyes. "Well, that was interesting."

"It would appear Mr. Dukhan has a personal stake in what you do, and with whom." Mauve's grin was delighted.

"Wrong," Amelia said. "I don't let men boss me around. Especially not men I don't know. Most especially not a man with an attitude."

Mauve reached under the hospital bed and pulled out Amelia's suitcase. She lifted it to the bed as Amelia swung her legs out from under the sheets and gingerly stood, fighting a wave of dizziness as she clutched at the hospital gown. "These things ought to be banned," she said. "They're hideous. I wonder what happened to my clothes."

Mauve shrugged. "They took you into the emergency room, and when you came out you were in this hospital getup. I can go check if you'd like."

Amelia shook her head. "Let it go. I just want to get out of here." Reaching for the suitcase, she started to unzip it, when she found a long slash in the leather. "Look at this," she said, calling Mauve's attention to the cut.

"When did that happen?" Mauve asked, fingering the slash that gave access to the interior of the bag. "Maybe it got caught on a machine in the baggage department."

"I didn't check the case at baggage. It was with me the entire time. I don't know when it could have gotten cut like that..." She looked at Mauve. "The man that poisoned me, he must have cut the bag. That's the only time anyone got close enough to do it."

She thought back to the incident. It had to have been the man who'd poisoned her. Reaching into her bag, she got clean clothes and quickly dressed in a silk sheath and sandals. Just as the doctor had predicted, she was feeling better and better.

"If getting your bag was the goal, then the man had a reason to poison you," Mauve said. "What did he think you were carrying in it? Money? Jewels?" She looked pointedly at the gold scarab on Amelia's neck. "Sometimes it isn't wise to wear expensive jewelry when you travel."

"Beth told me to wear this necklace. I thought it was so that you could identify me."

"As if I could miss you after listening to Beth talk about you for months on end," Mauve said, making a mock face. "Beth told you to wear the necklace?"

"When she sent it, the note said to wear it." Her fingers went to the scarab. "What kind of bug is it?"

Mauve rolled her eyes. ''Jeez, Amelia. It's the beetle of the tombs. It's sort of the scavenger bug.'' She hesitated. ''It feeds off the bodies.''

Amelia's hand dropped the pendant. ''Beth never had that kind of sense of humor.''

''It's an expensive piece. The gold looks pure and the craftsmanship is exquisite.''

''Maybe so, but it isn't exactly the kind of gift Beth would normally send to me.'' Amelia's long fingers went back to the pendant. She was troubled by the scarab and what it might represent. Had Beth been trying to send some kind of message? The best thing to do would be to find Beth and ask her in person. Her sister was a lot more important than even the premier French-perfume account.

''Ready?'' Mauve asked.

''Yes.'' Amelia took a deep breath. ''I suppose we're going to have to allow Mr. Dukhan to take us to the hotel he's selected for us.''

''Don't make it sound like such a sacrifice. The Abbula is a wonderful old hotel. Expensive, I might add. And as for Harad Dukhan, I think I could easily take a few orders from him.''

Amelia laughed despite herself. ''He is rather good-looking,'' she admitted.

''That, my dear, is the understatement of the year.''

''Okay, he's drop-dead gorgeous,'' Amelia conceded. ''But just because he's attractive doesn't mean he's a nice man.''

''Now that sounds like your sister, Beth. The old 'don't judge a book by its cover' routine. Honestly, if I'm going to be bamboozled by a man, I'd just prefer it to be a handsome, virile hunk, like Harad.''

''You have a point,'' Amelia said, lifting her suitcase. ''Let's continue with the bamboozling and see where it gets us.''

''Hey, if you decide on Harad, maybe you could point that doctor in my direction. He wasn't hard to look at, either.''

''Somehow, Mauve, I don't think you need any help in the men department.'' Amelia opened the door to find Harad standing only three feet away.

''Ladies,'' he said, walking into the room to lift the suitcase. He gave the slashed leather a long look.

''Amelia thinks it was the man who stuck her in the neck,'' Mauve supplied. ''Probably a thief.''

''An unsuccessful one,'' Amelia added. She walked out of the room, aware of Harad's gaze on her. Despite herself, she felt a shiver rush over her skin. He made her very aware that she was a woman.

HARAD CHOSE a table in the corner of the restaurant where he could watch the lobby. He'd reserved rooms for both Mauve and Amelia and they had gone to refresh themselves. First thing tomorrow, when he was sure Amelia was okay, he'd get her a flight out of town. He sipped a glass of wine as he tried to decide what to do with the two women for the remainder of the evening.

On the off chance that there was a night flight, he'd had his secretary check the airlines. If he could only reassure the blonde that Beth was okay, Amelia could be on a plane to Paris at ten in the morning. That was the scenario he preferred. No good could come of her visiting the lost City of Con. She was a danger to herself and others. Once she was airborne, he was relieved of all obligations to keep her safe. She could come back to visit at a better time.

He felt something under the table and reached down to stroke the black cat that twined through his legs. The last time he'd seen Familiar, the cat had been in the airport. Now he was at the Abbula. After listening to Omar and Beth talk about the cat, nothing about Familiar surprised Harad.

"Meow." Familiar hopped onto the chair beside Harad and looked pointedly at the dish of fresh butter.

"Lucky this is Egypt," Harad said as he buttered a piece of warm bread for the cat. "I don't think restaurants in America allow feline guests."

With great finesse, Familiar took the bread from his fingers. Harad was so engrossed in Familiar that he didn't notice the tall, slender woman who walked quietly up to the table.

"What is it with cats and Egyptians?"

Startled, Harad looked up to find Amelia watching him with humor.

"We honor the feline," he said, buttering another piece of bread and handing it to the cat. "Especially this feline. He played a large role in preventing injury to Beth." He could see that Amelia was both intrigued and a little skeptical. "Would you and Mauve care to have dinner with me? I'll fill you in on the details."

She hesitated, then gracefully sat in a chair opposite him. "Mauve is doing some vital work on a computer tonight and I get the feeling you're guarding me," she said as she settled a napkin onto her lap.

"I promised my brother that I would make sure you were safe." Another question popped out of his mouth, surprising him as much as her. "Does it bother you?" He signaled the waiter to bring another glass of wine.

Amelia quit playing with her napkin and looked directly into his eyes. "Yes and no."

When she didn't continue, he pressed. "Is there an explanation that comes with that answer?"

"I've fought a long time to be considered independent in a very tough business. For me to do my job effectively, I can't afford for anyone to look at me as someone who needs protection or to be cared for in any way." She spoke slowly, as if she was exploring her feelings as she went. "That's the yes part. The no part is that I have to admit, it is rather nice to know that someone cares what happens to me, even if it is someone who's obligated to care because of his brother."

Her smile took the sting out of her last words, and Harad found that he was smiling back at her. "Our siblings have woven an interesting web around us," he said. "You've come to protect your sister, who I might add seems completely capable of taking care of herself. And I'm here because of my brother. Soon you'll be safely on your way home. Perhaps we can simply let it go at that and enjoy dinner. I highly recommend the sea bass.''

Amelia pushed her unopened menu aside. ''Seeing as how you're my protector for the evening, I'll have the sea bass. By the way, my rooms are lovely. This is a wonderful old hotel.'' She leaned toward him, ''Even if they do allow cats to dine in the restaurant.''

Harad was captured by her warm smile and the hint of cleavage that was revealed by her forward movement. She wore a coral dress that fell smoothly over her slender figure. With her blond hair pulled casually into a bun, she was the perfect image of sophistication and poise. Yet there was a twinkle in her blue eyes that promised humor and mischief.

The waiter came to the table and Harad was about to order, when Familiar put a paw on the menu beside him.

''Meow!''

It was a demand not a request.

''I believe we'll have *three* sea bass,'' Harad said without blinking. ''And a saucer of heavy cream.''

AMELIA LEANED her wrists on the edge of the table to keep her hands still as Harad told her about her sister's involvement with criminals intent on using the ancient plant called the orbus to produce a potent drug that might give them an unfair advantage in controlling global events.

''I believe their goal was to use the drug to predict the future for political and financial gain,'' he said. ''But Beth and Omar figured out that several of

Beth's associates were involved in the plot. The criminals are in jail,'' he concluded.

''Beth was almost killed?'' Amelia knew she sounded breathless. ''When I got the packet she sent me, I knew something was wrong. But I never dreamed she was on the verge of being murdered.''

''My younger brother is a very capable man. He'll see to it that Beth is safe now.''

''Then all of the criminals were captured?''

Harad hesitated. ''The man who backed Beth's expedition, Nazar Bettina, could not be found. The authorities have discovered that no such man ever existed. We believe that John Gilmore, one of the scientists in Beth's employ, created the identity of Bettina to hide a cabal of wealthy Americans.''

''And those men will go unpunished?'' Amelia didn't try to hide her disappointment.

''I hope not,'' Harad said. ''But it is now between your government and mine. Mr. Gilmore will be strongly pressured to reveal the names, which so far he has refused to do. He claims he doesn't know who Nazar Bettina really is.''

''Is my sister safe?'' Amelia asked.

''She's very safe. Though Mr. Gilmore has so far refused to cooperate, the men who stood to gain from his deeds no longer have anything to gain. The plant that they sought has long been extinct. There is no longer an interest in your sister's explorations.''

''I'm still worried about her.'' Amelia's hand caught at the scarab pendant. ''She sent a note that said I should get to Alexandria as quickly as possible and to bring some photographs. Then I received this pendant so I would be recognized by the people who would meet me.''

''I knew nothing of the pendant,'' Harad said, his gaze taking in the piece. ''Omar sent me to meet you at the airport to make sure you understood everything was fine. And it is. Beth is safe and happy. You have my word. There is no need for you to change your business appointments. Beth's only regret was there wasn't time to get you to the wedding.''

''I'd give anything to be there, but Beth's happiness is all that's important.'' Amelia said. She couldn't help but notice Harad's hands. The fingers were long and tapered, and he used them with great eloquence as he talked. What would it be like to feel those fingers on her flesh? The thought was so erotic that she looked down at her plate. ''And this lost city that she was searching for, will she ever find it?''

Harad shrugged. ''That's between Omar and Beth. They must weigh the future.''

It was a diplomatic answer and gave Amelia time to compose herself and frame another question. ''Why is it that Omar is head of your people? You're the elder brother. Isn't it traditional for that role to go to the oldest son?''

''Or daughter, in the case of my people.'' Harad refilled her wineglass. ''With my people, the gift of prophecy was passed from mother to daughter. A female child was the greatest blessing of the gods.'' He gave a wry smile. ''I suppose you could say that I've grown up in a reverse culture.''

''That would be fascinating to experience,'' Amelia said. ''But you didn't answer my question. It was a good dodge, but not good enough.''

Harad laughed out loud, and Amelia found that she took great pleasure in his laughter. It had been a long, long time since she'd spent such an enjoyable evening.

''I wanted something other than the desert life. Omar loves the horses. He enjoys the sun and the restless nature of a nomadic tribe. He is also the keeper of the faith, and I'm not mocking him when I say that. Tradition, to him, is vital. To me, it is a hindrance. Once we both received our education in Paris I knew I would never return to the old way of life. I wanted to live in the city, to enjoy the luxuries that I could earn. He was the exact opposite. So I stepped aside and let the man best suited to rule take over. Instead of a desert leader, I studied architecture and then put together my own development company.''

Amelia played with the remains of her fish as Harad talked, but she was watching him closely. Though he was adept at casual talk, he didn't back away from revealing personal truths. In many ways, he was far more open about his feelings than anyone she'd met in ages. He was a fascinating and compelling man.

''You seem lost in thought, Ms. Corbet,'' he said, teasing her gently. ''Are you envisioning me astride a camel in the middle of sand?''

Amelia shook her head. ''Quite the contrary. I can

more easily see you on a Paris street or at an Austrian business table. If I were staying longer, I'd like to see some of the buildings you've developed.''

''My secretary did check on a flight to Paris for you,'' Harad said, reaching into his coat pocket to bring out the information. ''The first flight is at ten in the morning. I took the liberty of booking a ticket for you. You'll arrive in Paris in the evening. A car will be waiting for you there.''

Amelia arched her eyebrows. Everything had been going perfectly fine, until this. Harad had presumed too much. The one thing she simply couldn't abide was being treated as if she was six years old. ''Since I'm so close to Beth, I want to see her, even if I miss the wedding. I want to meet Omar.'' She didn't try to hide the implication of her last sentence. She wasn't leaving until she'd met Beth's husband.

Harad's features froze, then he recovered quickly. ''Beth and Omar are deep in the desert by now. It would be a long and arduous journey. You would do better to return for a real visit in a few months.''

''You could find a guide for me. Someone who could take me to them.'' She found that his resistance to the idea only made her more determined.

''I'm not sure that's a wise decision.''

''But it is *my* decision.''

Harad folded his napkin and placed it carefully on the table. He slipped several banknotes from his wallet and left them in the leather case that contained the bill. ''I highly recommend you reconsider.''

Amelia folded her napkin and stood also. The black

cat, who'd been busy eating until then, looked from one to the other.

"Meow."

"Will you provide me with a guide?" she asked.

"It would be difficult to find a seasoned guide for such a long journey on such short notice. Ms. Corbet, you must plan on being in the desert for at least two weeks. Such a trip requires tremendous preparation."

"I'm sure the concierge can help me arrange it," Amelia said. A deep flush had darkened Harad's cheeks, and his brown eyes were flecked with golden chips of anger. For a split second, Amelia regretted her rashness. She wasn't at all certain the concierge could arrange anything.

"Ms. Corbet, you're on your own. I'm afraid I can't help you. I can only wish you good luck." He bowed with a quick, efficient motion and walked away from her.

Chapter Three

How is it possible that someone who looks as if she was dropped straight from heaven can spoil one of the finest meals I've eaten in months? That delicious sea bass, which Harad ordered with only a tiny hint of prodding on my part, is rumbling around in my stomach now because Madame Taurus has given me indigestion. I'm going to call her Madame Taurus because she must have been born under the sign of the bull.

Amelia Corbet, for all of her blond hair and blue eyes, can curdle cream. That woman is so stubborn, if she drowned they'd have to search for her upstream. And I can see the look in her eyes. She's going to insist on going into the desert. She's going to hire a guide and take off across the sand like it's some kind of picnic.

The more Harad argues with her, the more determined she's going to become. He finally caught on to that—he just zipped his lip and walked away. Washed his hands of the whole situation, I dare say.

So that leaves me to look out for Madame Taurus.

Boy, I've worked with some strong women in my time, but I don't think a single one of them could hold a candle to Amelia Corbet. Darth Vader would consider backing up from her.

All of this might be amusing, except I see a terrible picture in my future. It involves a horse, sand, sun, thirst and a lot of other unpleasant things. Most of the time, I feel my black suit is the purrfect attire for any occasion. There is one place, though, for which I am not properly dressed, and that is the dang-blasted desert.

I have no choice but to go. Eleanor and Peter are going to be fried at me. They've warned me that they won't wait for me. I know that isn't true, but I'm also a realist. How long can they wait? Harad said a two-week excursion. Something tells me I'd better get my name and address sewn into my underfur. I'm going to be on my own.

Thanks to all this tension, my tummy feels like World War II is being replayed inside. I need an Alka-Seltzer. Oh, this is not my idea of fun, and I'm not even getting paid for all this worry.

Time to get moving. Amelia is headed up to her room, and I'd better keep an eye on her. She's trouble on two very lovely legs. This is going to be a long, long night.

THE EVENING had turned slightly cool, and Harad was thankful for the sea breeze against his heated face. He'd been so angry at Amelia that he had walked away before he said something he would regret. There were plenty of things he'd wanted to say—things about her stupidity and arrogance and stubbornness. But those were things best left unvoiced. For all her tough business experience, Amelia was a pampered American. It would take only a day or two in the desert to make her change her mind.

At the thought of her tired and sore from the rolling git of a camel, he found a glimmer of satisfaction. A bit of hardship might soften her tough attitude. It didn't take a brain surgeon to see that Amelia Corbet was a woman used to the finer things in life.

She'd been so perfectly turned out at dinner. The coral of the dress was matched by her lipstick and nail polish. The hint of eye shadow had brightened the crystal blue of her eyes. That moment, when she'd leaned forward, caught up in his story, he'd caught a glimpse of cleavage, and the ivory sheen of her skin had made him want to press his lips there. He could still smell the delicate perfume she wore, warmed by her body heat. Even the memory of it was powerful enough to make him close his eyes for a moment.

At the thought of kissing her, his blood grew more heated, and he forced himself to walk. The last thing he needed was to stand around on a street corner and fantasize about a spoiled American woman who was girding her loins to make his next two weeks a living misery.

He thought briefly of finding a local guide to take her, but there was no one he trusted. There were many good guides, but none who would have the fortitude to lead Amelia to the conclusion she needed to draw—Paris was where she ought to be. He found himself caught on the horns of a dilemma. Though Beth would surely want to see her sister, especially when she and Omar celebrated their wedding, Harad wasn't certain that Amelia could be trusted with the secret location of the lost City of Con. It would be best for all if Amelia came to visit when Beth and Omar returned to Alexandria.

Omar had decided to risk that knowledge with Beth, but Harad was not willing to do the same with Amelia. He'd put his heritage and his people in second place once before, when he'd refused the role of leader. He would not do it a second time.

The immediate problem was the desert trip. He would have to trick Amelia into accepting him as a guide. She trusted him less than he trusted her—and he smiled at that thought.

How to convince her? Amelia was far too smart to simply sign on to the idea that he'd changed his mind and decided to follow her orders. Circumstances would have to be such that when he appeared at her campsite, it would be as her rescuer. At the thought of her, blue eyes filled with gratitude, he increased the pace of his walking. That would be a first for Amelia Corbet. He'd be willing to wager a large sum that she'd never been grateful to a man for a single thing in her life.

It was time to change that.

There was little time for bemoaning what had to be done, so he used his cell phone to call his car and driver and began to make preparations for the trip.

In the center of town was a man who provided camels and equipment for excursions into the desert. Harad had done business with him before and knew the animals he leased were healthy and well cared for. Though it was not regular business hours, Harad had his driver go there. He would also need tents and supplies—and he would keep the receipts. Somewhere along the way, Amelia Corbet had to learn that her hardheadedness was a costly vice.

CHEEKS STILL red with righteous indignation, Amelia closed the door of her suite none too gently. She saw the swinging door barely miss the black cat's tail as he darted into her room. The creature had followed her from the restaurant and had plopped himself in the middle of her bed, as if it was his right.

"I'm not a pushover like the Egyptians," she warned him.

The black cat stared her right in the eyes and used his back legs to push her suitcase onto the floor. The leather case hit the floor with an impressive smack.

"Hey!" She started walking toward him with the intention of picking him up and putting him out of the room. His tail flicked once as he reclined, watching her. When she reached out to pick him up, she heard a low, deadly growl. The sound halted her in her tracks. She'd never heard anything more adamant.

Amelia turned abruptly and reached for the telephone. Just as she started to dial the front desk for assistance with cat removal, Familiar sprang to his feet and caught the rotary dial with his sharp claws. He gave a low growl of warning.

Very slowly Amelia lowered the phone back into its cradle. She stared into the cat's golden gaze. "I don't know what you want, but you can't sleep on the bed."

The cat walked back across the bed, turned in a circle once and then settled into a ball. In what seemed like seconds, he was sound asleep and purring.

Amelia sat on the edge of the bed and examined the feline. She'd never met an animal with such presence. J.J. was a sweet and lovable mutt, but he bent over backward to please her. This cat was another matter. She had the distinct impression that he had it fully in mind to bend *her* to *his* will.

"We'll see about that," she whispered softly. The cat's whiskers twitched and he opened his eyes. His golden-green gaze was calm, and then he yawned.

Amelia wanted to tell the cat that he could go straight to Hades, but she couldn't bring herself to continue to talk to the animal. Even Harad, a man with a multimillion-dollar business, spoke to Familiar as if he thought the cat actually understood. It was ridiculous. The cat might be intuitive and somehow skilled in showing up at the right place at the right time, but it was completely foolish to believe the feline understood language.

Reaching into her purse, she pulled out Dr. Kaffar Mosheen's business card. She tapped it against the bedside table.

"I wonder if there's another phone around here," she mused out loud, casting sidelong glances at the sleeping cat to see how he reacted. When Familiar made no move to thwart her efforts, she dialed the doctor. "Stupid cat. He doesn't understand a thing," she muttered under her breath as she waited for the doctor to answer.

Amelia identified herself and heard the gratifying intake of breath on the other end of the line. "I have an hour or so this evening if you'd still like to talk to me about the poisoning," she said. "I'm staying at the Abbula."

"Lovely old hotel," he said. "I'll be there in half an hour. We could meet—"

"In the bar," Amelia supplied. "I'll be waiting for you." She made it a practice never to let a man make all the decisions. It was good training for them, and for her.

She stood up, smoothed her dress over her hips, checked her reflection in the mirror and started out the door. She turned back to see if the cat was still asleep on the bed.

To her total surprise, the bed was empty. She stared at it a moment. Familiar had vanished. Shaking her head, she walked out of the room and found the cat already waiting for her in the hall. Like some kind of magician, he'd slipped through the door just as she opened it. He led the way to the elevators. As soon as they were in the lobby, he ran into the bar. When she walked in, she found him sitting on a bar stool with a large saucer of cold milk in front of him. In the four seconds he'd been ahead of her, Familiar had somehow managed to charm the burly bartender.

Disgusted, Amelia sat as far from the cat as she could. It was impossible, but it did seem as if he'd understood her conversation on the phone. Either that or he had a serious drinking problem.

All thoughts of Familiar left her head, though, when Kaffar Mosheen walked into the bar. He'd forsaken his white coat, and he wore khakis and a cotton pullover. The pale yellow of the shirt gave his complexion a warm glow. As he took a bar stool beside her, he waved the bartender over.

"Two vodka martinis," he said, "alcohol should be okay if your headache's gone."

"Make that one vodka martini and one iced tea," Amelia said. She turned to Kaffar. "My headache is gone, but I'd rather have tea. You look very different without your lab coat."

"I hope I'm very different," he said, smiling. "Earlier today, you were a patient. Now you are a lovely woman that I hope to impress. Still, I must ask how you feel?"

Amelia laughed. One thing she could say about Alexandria—she'd never met more charming men. She thought of Harad and felt her throat go dry. Even as her body tingled at the thought of him, she smiled at the doctor.

"I'm good as new.

"Tell me about your work," she said, sipping the drink the bartender had put in front of her.

The doctor began to talk of his research on plants

used in herbal remedies to stop smoking. Amelia listened intently, but she was aware of the black cat walking along the top of the bar in her general direction.

When he was in front of Dr. Mosheen, he lifted a big paw and held it aloft for a few seconds. With one swipe, he sent the martini tumbling off the bar and into the doctor's lap.

Kaffar Mosheen calmly stood. Using a napkin from the bar, he blotted the liquid from his slacks. "My countrymen have a great reverence for the cat," he said, his voice calm and easy. His eyes held anger. "But I personally hate them. They carry disease. They are a plague upon the city." He tossed the damp napkin at the black cat's head. "I would have every single one of them deported or destroyed."

Amelia placed her drink on the bar. "Don't you think that's just a bit of an overreaction? I'm not all that fond of cats, but they aren't that bad."

Dr. Mosheen accepted the new drink the bartender brought him. "Perhaps you are right." He smiled. "Perhaps we should simply create a cat-free zone." He reached over the bar and touched Amelia's hand. "Let's not let a silly accident spoil our chat. Now tell me about your work."

Amelia gave a rough outline of the work she did for Bretzel and Burke, explaining that she was on her way to Paris as soon as she left Alexandria.

"And when will that be?" Kaffar asked.

"I'm not certain." Amelia found that her resolve to track her sister into the desert had waned. The more she thought about the adventure, the less she liked it. Harad's high-handed treatment had gotten her dander up, but now she wasn't certain she wanted to follow through. She couldn't make the wedding, so perhaps a planned visit—in town—would be better.

"If you're staying through tomorrow, perhaps I could drive you to Cairo. There are many things to see. Or we could explore the pyramids. Certainly you can't visit Egypt and not see the Sphinx or the Great Pyramid."

Amelia was relieved to see Mauve enter the bar. She didn't have an answer for the doctor. He was an attractive man and the idea of sightseeing with him held appeal, but her heart really wasn't in the game. If she didn't chase down Beth, she needed to head to Paris. She stood and waved the redhead over to them. "Could I let you know tomorrow?" Amelia asked the doctor.

"Certainly." He rose smoothly to his feet as Mauve joined them. After another twenty minutes of chitchat, Amelia excused herself, pleading exhaustion from her illness. Mauve and the doctor were deep in conversation. Just as she was turning to go, she winked at Mauve and gave her a thumb's-up sign.

She was smiling to herself when she walked across the lobby. She'd left Mauve a clear field. Now it was up to the redhead to play the game.

HARAD ARRIVED BACK in the lobby of the Abbula just in time to see Amelia in the bar, shaking Dr. Kaffar Mosheen's hand. Mauve was there, too, staring up at the doctor with obvious interest. Still, jealousy made Harad's back tighten and his fists clench. The good doctor had wasted no time in moving in on Amelia. Then he remembered that Dr. Mosheen hadn't known where Amelia was staying. Obviously she had called him.

Harad stepped behind a column in the lobby to avoid detection. He'd come to tell Amelia that the arrangements for her excursion had been made. Standing in the lobby, watching the beautiful blonde walk past him, Harad knew that his motivation had been to see Amelia again. He could have telephoned the information to her, but telling her in person was a good reason to see her. And no matter how much he tried to deny it to himself, he wanted to see her.

He waited until she had time to get to her room, then he went to a hotel phone and dialed her number. She answered quickly, and he wondered if it was because she thought the doctor might be asking her to return. Another stab of feeling pricked him. The sensation was disorienting. He'd known a lot of beautiful women in the past, but none had ignited the fiery dagger of jealousy.

It had to be that Amelia was a challenge. That had to be the factor in his irrational emotions. He settled on that as he told her that he was in the lobby with news and documents for her, then waited. Her answer would tell him a lot about her.

"I'm not sleepy," she said. "Why don't you come up and tell me?"

He smiled as he hung up the phone and went to

the elevator. It would seem Amelia had no interest in returning to the lobby. She'd left Kaffar Mosheen with Mauve. Harad couldn't be certain of her exact reason, but he knew that it was a good sign as far as her intentions toward the doctor were concerned. He felt as if he'd gained ground in the battle.

Tapping on her door, he waited until she opened it. She was still dressed in the coral sheath, and she nodded toward a grouping of seats in the sitting room of the suite he'd rented for her.

"So, you found a guide for me?" she asked.

He thought he detected some reservation in her voice. Perhaps she was reconsidering.

"My conscience wouldn't allow me to abandon you. The desert can be deadly. I gave Omar my word I would make sure you were safe. I've found a guide. He's a trustworthy man, and he has the knowledge and resources to take you to Omar and Beth."

Amelia's face remained emotionless. "Thank you, Harad. It was kind of you to go to that trouble, and to do it so quickly."

He nodded. "I still would not advise you to make this trip," he said. "It's a difficult journey, and dangerous. Not because of bandits or wild beasts. It is simply the endless sand and sun. A tiny miscalculation, and you could end up wandering for days." He paused. "Or forever."

His words were working on the chink in Amelia's determination. If he judged it just right, he might be able to let her talk herself out of the entire misadventure.

"The guide you hired is reliable, though?"

"Yes, the very best. I was lucky he hadn't already been engaged. But he is quite expensive. I warn you, you get what you pay for in this business, and it's always best to purchase the finest. In equipment and personnel."

"Yes." She went to her purse and brought out a checkbook. "I'll gladly reimburse you."

He pulled the bills from his pocket and handed them to her. With a little help from Tep the guide, he'd padded them quite successfully. Once Amelia conceded the trip, he would personally refund all of her money.

He saw her eyebrows lift at the figure. "Ten *thousand* dollars?"

"Yes, he gave me a very good price, don't you think?"

"I had no idea. I thought—" She bit off the rest of the sentence.

It was hard for Harad not to grin. "You will have Tep the guide, and one additional man. This amount will also cover all provisions, tents and camels."

"Camels?" Amelia's head snapped up. "I thought there were horses. Those Arabians. You know, *The Black Stallion, King of the Wind,* that kind of horse."

"Unfortunately, this trip might be too arduous for a horse," he continued to fib. "The camel has more stamina. More ability to survive if you should become lost. The hump. Perhaps you remember studying camels in some of your science classes." He found he was having a delightful time, even if his conscience nagged at him. Still, his first priority was to protect his people.

"There are air searches, should someone become lost, right?"

"They are seldom successful. The desert is so vast. There are no landmarks. It makes air searches next to impossible. Of course, we would try..." He let his sentence fall away then stood. "Now I must go. The directions are written out for you. Be at that address at dawn."

"Dawn?"

"An early start puts you that much ahead of the blaze of the sun. I believe the hotel shops are still open. If I were you, I'd invest in all the sunblock they have. Your skin is so fair. The sun here is unkind to such skin. After two weeks, you'll look much older. It should assist you in your professional life. I understand that older women are given more respect." He went to her, lifted her hand and kissed it gently. "Good luck, Amelia Corbet. It was a pleasure to meet you."

He hurried out of the room before he burst into laughter. Maybe for the first time in her life, Amelia Corbet was *behind* the eight ball instead of aiming it at someone else.

Chapter Four

Dawn was just breaking in the eastern sky as Amelia got out of the taxi on the outskirts of Alexandria. Instead of the spices of the city, she caught the scent of horses and leather. The wind tugged gently at her white cotton blouse. To the south was the wide-open vista of the desert. She was at the right place.

The low, stucco building was the only place to go, and she paid the cabbie and lugged her recently purchased backpack over to the building and leaned it against the wall. Her shopping spree had been hasty and limited to the hotel shops, but she'd managed to find jeans and a few cotton blouses.

She was hesitating about leaving the backpack with her important papers against the wall, when the whinny of a horse caught her attention. She wished she wasn't headed across the desert on a camel. She loved horses. In fact, she'd been the top jumper in the stables where she'd taken lessons years ago. That memory made her think of Beth, who also rode, but with a more conservative approach.

It would be good to see Beth. Far too much time—

almost six months—had passed since they'd been together. That was what she had to focus on, not the camels or the hot sun or the desert. She looked again at the vast expanse of rolling waves of sand. The sun had begun to highlight the dunes with pink and gold, and Amelia was captured by the beauty of a place she'd never thought could be beautiful. To her the word *desert* had always meant thirst, burning heat and death. *Untamed* was the word that now came to mind. It was a wild beauty that the desert claimed.

And it was a little intimidating. Well, a lot intimidating. She could admit that, as long as no one was listening to her thoughts.

She walked into the building and was instantly captured by the beauty of the horses. A low whinny drew her to the first stall. "What a beauty," she whispered to a gray mare. She was petting the horse's forehead when she heard footsteps behind her.

"Ms. Corbet," the man said, bowing. "I am Tep." He smiled at her from beneath a white headdress. His flowing robes could not conceal the fact that he was tall and thin.

"You must come this way," Tep said, taking her elbow and steering her through the stables and to the back. "I have retrieved the pack you left out front. All is ready and we must depart."

Amelia saw the camels instantly. There were five of them, two standing and three kneeling on the ground. Without even giving her a chance to hesitate, Tep pushed her toward one of the kneeling camels and in a matter of thirty seconds she was on its back.

The animal rudely complained as Tep forced it to its feet.

Amelia forgot about everything except hanging on to the wooden cradle that passed for a saddle. The rocking motion of the animal made it impossible to sit, and she hung on for dear life. Though Tep had put some rope reins in her hand, she could neither steer nor slow her camel as it began to run toward the desert.

''Halt! Halt!'' Tep called after her. ''Pull the ropes!'' he cried.

''I am. It isn't doing any good!'' she yelled back, hauling on the reins. Then she didn't bother trying to yell anything as the camel hurled itself away from civilization and into the heart of the desert.

Amelia knew that she'd made a serious mistake. Her pride and stubbornness had led her to a sorry pass, and now she was about to experience the consequences.

SITTING ASTRIDE his Arabian stallion, Harad laughed out loud as he followed the progress of Amelia's runaway camel through binoculars. Tep was as good as his word. He'd promised that he had a young camel that would give Amelia the ride of her life.

He laughed again as the camel hung a sharp right and nearly unseated Amelia. She was hanging on with all of her strength, and in a matter of a few hours she would sincerely regret her decision to storm into the desert. Ah, he would savor the moment of sweet defeat when he went to rescue her and bring her back to Alexandria. And hopefully on her way home to safety.

Harad scanned the remainder of Amelia's traveling party and wasn't surprised to see a wicker basket strapped to the back of the last camel. The lid popped up slightly and he saw Familiar's head peep out. The cat had attached himself to Amelia, just as he had to Beth. Harad had no explanation for it, and he didn't need one. Cats were extraordinary creatures, and it only stood to reason that some were more exceptional than others. Familiar fell into that category. The cat would watch out for Amelia for the next forty-eight hours as Tep softened her up and prepared her to welcome Harad as her savior.

Laughing out loud, he turned his horse and headed back to the stables. Tep would run Amelia around in circles in the desert for the next two days. Once she believed she was lost and in a hopeless situation, he would appear. Amelia would agree to come back another time, and the City of Con would be safe. And although he'd made plans with Tep to check in at certain points to ensure Amelia's safety, he wouldn't be stuck with her twenty-four hours a day. It was a brilliant plan, even if he'd conceived of it himself.

As for himself, he had business to attend to in Alexandria. He was meeting several foreign businessmen to discuss an international merger on a building in Cairo that would become the central focus of Middle Eastern contemporary art. He wanted to be part of that building, a place that would preserve for the future the creativity of the present.

He groomed his gray stallion, Pooldar, and called his car and driver. As they entered the heart of Alexandria, the city was already alive. Merchants were putting their wares out in kiosks in the open market, and those who ran the large, more European department stores were unfolding awnings that had been closed for the night.

In front of Dukhan Enterprises, Harad got out of the car. He stopped to buy two cups of fresh coffee and a selection of fresh rolls, carrying them with him to his office. Both Tut, his cat, and his executive assistant were there to greet him. His secretary was on vacation.

"What are you up to?" Marie Johnson asked. "And don't bother to deny it. I see that look in your eyes. You're either on a hot deal or you're into some mischief."

"Mischief," he answered. Marie had been an American diplomat's wife. The marriage had ended, and Harad had hired the petite brunette at a salary that exceeded her ex-husband's. She spoke four languages and could run the most complicated set of numbers in her head. She was his most valuable secret weapon in the business world.

"I pity the fool that ends up in your gun sights," she said.

"No harm will come of this," he assured her. "Just a little bit of damaged pride and possibly a bruised posterior."

Marie held up a hand. "TMI—that's too much information. Don't tell me another thing. I don't want to be called as a witness against you."

Laughing, Harad handed her a cup of coffee and the bag of fresh buns. "If I could only teach you to make coffee," he said.

"Watch it, buster. I don't make coffee, and I don't dust."

Marie had grown up with five brothers. It was one of Harad's delights to hear some of her "tough" expressions.

"Many of my business associates are interested in proposing marriage to you until I tell them the long list of things you will not do. No coffee, no dusting, no running errands, no laundry, no vacuuming. They decide then that you would be a wife with too much time on her hands."

"Tell them when they want a partner instead of a servant to give me a call." Marie went to her desk. "On a less personal level, you had a call this morning from a Dr. Mosheen. He said something about some blood tests."

Harad felt his lighthearted mood evaporate. Mosheen again. He took the slip of paper from Marie's hand.

"What's wrong?" she asked, instantly recognizing the change in him.

"What did he say about the blood tests?"

Marie thought. "He said that something else had shown up and that he was looking for Amelia Corbet."

"Thanks." Harad took the number and went to his

private office. Tut followed him and jumped into his lap as he placed the call.

Kaffar Mosheen was making rounds, but he came on the line quickly.

"I'm searching for Amelia," he said. "The blood work looked perfect yesterday, but there were some changes this morning."

"Can you be more specific?" Harad asked.

"Ms. Corbet should return to the hospital for more tests. I can't be more specific."

"Is this life-threatening?" Harad pressed. He could get Amelia back to the hospital, but it would take at least a day.

"Most likely not, but it would be best to get Ms. Corbet back here as soon as possible," Mosheen said, his voice calm and soothing. "There is an irregularity in the tests. I have tried to call her hotel, and she has checked out, but she left some things at the desk. I assumed she is returning there?"

"Yes, in a day or so."

"It would be most helpful to see her immediately." The doctor's voice was firm.

"I'll find her," Harad said.

"She is in the city?" Mosheen pressed.

"She's on an excursion. I can locate her."

"This could be nothing," Mosheen said. "It is only that I don't wish to run any chances. I may inconvenience Amelia by interrupting her excursion, but I think it is better to be safe than sorry."

"I couldn't agree more," Harad said. He checked his watch. He had twenty minutes before his meeting Five men were flying in from all over the Middle East.

"Shall I telephone Amelia at the hotel a little later?" Mosheen asked. "As you may know, I have a special interest in Amelia's care. And she's a beautiful woman."

"I'll take care of it." Harad was surprised at the terseness in his voice.

"Shall I wait here in the hospital for her?"

"No, it may take me some time to find her."

"Please page me as soon as she returns," Mosheen said, and gave Harad his number.

AMELIA WOULD never have believed a person could get seasick in the desert, but waves of nausea crested over her as the camel continued its endless rolling gait and the miles of sand extended to the horizon.

This trip was a mistake. All she had to do was call out to Tep that she'd changed her mind. He could keep the money, she simply wanted to go back to Alexandria. Back to the Abbula and a hot bath, cool sheets and a bottle of cold soda.

The only good thing that could be said about the morning was that her camel had finally grown tired of running away with her and was now following the others with a more docile attitude. For the moment.

"We are resting," Tep said as he rode up beside her. His forehead creased. "You are sick?"

"Hungry," she said, hoping it was true. She hadn't eaten breakfast, and it was well past noon.

Tep signaled his associate to stop and they circled

the camels. The other man hopped to the ground and began unpacking things from one of the riderless camels. Amelia fleetingly considered offering to help but decided against it. Olli, her camel, was kneeling, but she wasn't certain she'd be able to dismount. Her butt and thighs were killing her.

Tep's strong hand offered assistance as she finally dismounted, barely able to suppress a groan.

"We will rest," he said, pointing for her to sit in the small shadow that the camel cast. "We have many, many miles to go. We cannot stay here long."

Amelia collapsed against Olli, who now seemed completely content to be friendly. It occurred to her that he was finally worn out. He'd spit at her, kicked the other camels, and twice tried to bite Tep.

The other man, who had not been introduced, brought her water and a flat sandwich. He wore his headdress low on his forehead, the long sides concealing most of his face from the burning sun. Amelia had slathered her face with sunblock, but she could still feel the burning rays. Maybe one of the men would show her how to fashion something like they wore to cover her head.

She didn't recognize anything in her sandwich and didn't care. She was starving. She wolfed it down and was considering asking for another when Tep signaled for them to rise.

"We must go."

It wasn't a negotiable point, Amelia realized. She rose to her feet and climbed back on top of Olli. Complaining loudly, he got to his feet. Instead of running away, as she expected, he waited for the others.

Amelia's path to success in the highly competitive advertising world had been fraught with obstacles. She'd learned the value of a positive philosophy. On the bright side, she could say that things actually were improving.

Since Olli was being so cooperative, she guided him to fall into line behind one of the pack camels. She'd noticed the wicker basket when they first started, and she'd heard Tep talking to the basket. The first thought that crossed her mind was snake. But then, those baskets were round not square. This was more like a picnic basket.

Nudging Olli to a slightly faster pace, she inched closer to the pack animal. She was curious, but focusing on the basket was more a way to pass time than anything else. She could play guessing games as to what it might contain.

"Dried dates," she said out loud. But Tep wouldn't talk to dates. Was there something alive in the basket? A mongoose? What other types of animals were native to the desert? She'd never been much of a student of science or geography.

When the lid of the basket popped up, Amelia held her breath. "I don't believe this," she said as she recognized the black cat. "How did you manage this?"

"Meow!"

Familiar sounded about as happy as she felt. Strangely enough, though, she was glad to see the cat. At least she'd have another creature to suffer with.

"If we get back to Alexandria, I'll treat you to the biggest steak or the freshest seafood dinner available," she said, realizing she, too, was now talking to the cat. "We'll do that right after I find a good shrink to talk to."

She saw the cat swivel his attention from her to the distance. At first she wasn't certain she saw anything. Then she realized someone, or something, was coming down the nearest dune at a breakneck pace. It took her a moment longer to be able to distinguish two riders on horseback headed straight toward them. It didn't cross her mind that this might not be a good thing until she felt Olli lurch forward from the sharp slap that Tep had given him on the rump.

"Bandits!" Tep cried. "Bandits! They'll take you hostage and sell you into white slavery!" He hit the camel again. "Run!"

Olli brayed angrily and began a desperate lurching run.

Amelia leaned forward in the saddle and tried to give Olli as much freedom of movement as she could. No matter how hard the camel ran, though, the horsemen were gaining on her.

She was far ahead of Tep and his assistant. The pack camels had stopped, their tethers dangling on the ground. Amelia made no effort to guide Olli because she had no idea where she was headed. The only sense of direction she had was the waning sun. She was headed into it, and that's what she'd have to remember. It would be the only lead she had if she was lucky enough to have an opportunity to try and get home.

The words *white slavery* bounced in her brain. She'd read accounts of women who were allegedly abducted in foreign countries, but she'd always thought of them as high-school girls or college kids—younger women who were easy victims.

The terrible truth came home to her. Only two people knew where she was—Harad and Mauve. She'd refused to allow the redhead to accompany her, and now she was both glad and sorry. With Mauve, at least she'd have an ally. But it would also mean that the scientist would face the same ugly fate that was chasing after her.

She glanced back and felt her heart almost stop. Two of the men were only fifty yards behind her, their horses galloping over the sand. She could see nothing of their faces. They were covered by the flowing material that covered their heads. But she saw the weapons at their sides.

Two hundred yards back, Tep and his assistant were standing on the ground, their hands in the air as the third bandit held them at gunpoint.

She leaned closer to the camel's back and prayed for more speed. She was not surprised, though, when one of the horses drew abreast of Olli and a hand reached out to grab the reins near his nose.

With a quick jerk, the man pulled Olli to a standstill.

"Another desert flower to be plucked," the man said, laughing. He turned to his friend. "Look what we have, a pretty, pale flower of great value."

Chapter Five

Harad circled Pooldar in the sand and checked the map he held in his hand. He'd carefully plotted the circular route that Tep would take to keep Amelia close to Alexandria yet far enough into the desert so that she wouldn't suspect she was being manipulated.

He checked the east—the direction he expected them to come from. The first star could be seen in the slowly darkening sky. There was no sign of the small convoy.

A bad feeling crept over Harad. Something had happened. Something unexpected. Tep was a reliable man. He'd fully understood his assignment, and in the past he'd never failed to carry out one of Harad's requests.

Harad thought he might be seeing things when he saw two bedraggled men walking across the sand toward him. One man stumbled and the other grabbed his elbow and held him upright. Using the binoculars, Harad identified Tep and his assistant. Both men had been beaten.

Squeezing lightly with his legs, Harad felt Pooldar

surge beneath him as the powerful horse took off at a full gallop toward the men. With each stride, Harad felt his blood pulsing.

"Tep!" he called when he was within hailing distance. The man looked up and waved wearily.

Harad was beside them quickly. He leaped from his horse and grasped Tep by the shoulders. "What happened? Where is Amelia?"

"Bandits," Tep said, shaking his head. "They stole the camels and the woman."

"How badly are you hurt?" Harad asked.

"Not so bad." Tep rubbed his temple where a gash had bled down his face. "They could have killed us, but they didn't. They wanted the woman and the camels. We tried to resist them."

"Did you recognize any of them?" he asked, clinging to a slim hope that Tep would know at least the tribe where the bandits had come from. It would be a starting place.

Tep shook his head. "There was no distinctive clothing, no way to identify them. I'd never seen them before."

"How did they find you?"

"They came out of the dunes. It was as if they were laying in wait for us."

Harad considered that statement. "Did you tell anyone you were going to be taking Ms. Corbet out today?"

"Only Luth," he said, indicating the other man. "I told him only this morning. He had no time to speak to anyone, and he wouldn't do such a thing."

Harad wasn't so certain about that, but when he looked at the assistant, he was inclined to believe Tep. The man had been hit even harder than his boss. He still seemed a little dazed.

Harad dismounted and helped Tep and Luth up on Pooldar. Both men protested, but he ignored them. By Harad's best calculations, they were at least four miles from the stables. It was going to be a long, hot walk and time was precious. His impulse was to pursue the men who'd abducted Amelia, but he couldn't leave Tep and Luth in the desert without any means of transportation. He had to take them back to the city and then mount a search for Amelia.

Clucking to the stallion to move forward, he began the journey back to town.

AT FIRST AMELIA tried going limp. The taller man had her in his grasp and was tugging her arms behind her back. He was needlessly rough. Instead of fighting, she simply dropped to the ground, dead weight.

It was not the most brilliant tactic.

She felt the rope bite into her wrists as he tightly tied her hands behind her back. With a heave he swung her up and into the saddle of one of the horses. The other man tied all five camels in a line together.

Tep and his assistant lay in the sand. She knew they weren't dead, but they'd been savagely beaten when they'd tried to resist the bandits.

Amelia had considered fighting, but she had no doubt the bandits would beat her as severely as Tep and Luth. She should have resisted, though. She should have at least inflicted some damage. Now she was tied like a cowboy's prize heifer. At least she'd been given a horse to ride instead of the recalcitrant Olli.

The men spoke together in a tongue she didn't understand, but she caught the meaning as one slapped her horse's rump and began to herd the camels into a loping walk. With her hands behind her back, Amelia had to fight to keep her balance in the saddle. If only she could get her hands free, she'd give the men a run for their money. She was an excellent rider and she judged the horse beneath her to be of great spirit and stamina.

Even as she plotted escape, she knew it was a mind game she played to keep her fears at bay. She'd been captured by men who viewed her as nothing more than a camel. She was a creature to be sold for profit. What happened to her was of no concern to the men.

The very idea of it was terrifying.

Why hadn't she listened to Harad? She caught an image of him in her mind, and she would have given almost anything to see his face. Though he might smirk and torment her, she sensed he would also be able to get her out of the mess she was in.

The men spoke to each other and laughed, and Amelia felt their eyes on her. She'd never in her life feared for her own physical safety. It was a new and bitter sensation.

"My family is very wealthy," she said slowly. They spoke English. She'd heard them. "They'll pay a lot more money to have me returned than anyone else would."

"Ransom?" one man said. He poked the other in the side and they both laughed. "No, I think there is a man in Istanbul who will pay the premium price for you. He has been searching for a woman like you for a long time. He will be very grateful to us and will reward us with many pounds."

"My family will pay more," Amelia insisted. "They'll pay double whatever you can get anywhere else. I swear to you."

The men only laughed and prodded the beasts of burden to a faster pace. Amelia had to concentrate on riding to keep from falling off. At least she'd spoken to her captors. They had replied. It was small progress. Over time, though, she would have to make them reconsider. She only hoped that she had time before they got to whatever settlement they called headquarters. Instinctively, she knew her odds were best with the two men alone.

I DON'T BELIEVE THIS. Where's Harrison Ford? Where are the cameras? I didn't hear anyone calling out, "Action!" But surely this must be a movie. It is impossible that I'm riding in a wicker basket on the back of a camel being led to who knows where by two white slavers. I am almost tempted to jump out right here and now. But I can't leave Amelia to her fate.

She was told. She was warned. She was requested not to go into the desert. But would she listen? No-o-o-o-o! So now I find myself marched off into the burning hot sand in the middle of the summer. And to top it all off, Amelia doesn't even respect me.

Gads. This is a bitter pill.

So the two abductors have done this before. They're professionals. Desert bandits. Pirates of the sand. If I weren't so put out with Amelia, I might find this slightly interesting. Eleanor and Peter will be worried sick. I'm more than a little worried.

Just because Egyptians, in general, worship felines, doesn't mean that everyone follows that practice. These two guys might find kitty target practice to be a lot of fun.

I'm going to have to take some kind of action. I should have done something to thwart this entire misadventure, but I thought Harad was on the case. In the back of my mind, I assumed he was somehow responsible for the desert abduction. Boy, was I wrong. But I'm still betting on Harad. He's my ace in the hole. I can only hope that right this minute he's launching a search for us.

At the first rest break, I'm going to come out of my basket and hitch a ride on the back of Amelia's horse. If she gives me one contemptuous look, I'm going to bite her. Her hands are tied with rope. Perhaps I can manage to loosen her bonds enough so that she can get free. It's not actually a plan, but it is a step. After that, we'll have to play it by ear. I only hope Amelia's stubbornness hasn't made her tone deaf.

WHEN TEP'S WIFE assured him that neither man was seriously injured, Harad jumped into his car and ordered the driver to take him to his office. Two things were gnawing at him.

From the way Tep had described the attack, it seemed almost as if the two bandits had been lying in wait. But in the vast stretches of the desert, why would any bandits come so close to the city, and why would they suspect that anyone would travel in that particular area? The route Harad had drawn for Tep to follow was a large circle. It led nowhere. Bandits normally lurked along the traditional trade routes—the paths taken by tourists and large expeditions.

The second area of concern was that Tep said the men spoke English. Many Bedouins were bi- or even trilingual. The nomadic cultures of the Middle East had crossed land boundaries for many years. Bartering and trading had necessitated a fluency in language—but English was not normally included.

Harad's concerns centered on the evidence that the bandits were professionals—and had been sent specifically to abduct Amelia.

But why?

She was a wealthy American professional. True. But the purpose of the bandits didn't seem to be ransom. Tep had overheard them say that Amelia would bring a high price. That meant she was being sold for her looks. She, herself, was of no value.

If ransom was ruled out, why would someone deliberately abduct a wealthy American woman? The white slavers normally preyed upon young girls and women who could be taken without too much fuss.

The abduction of Amelia Corbet would cause a lot of heat.

Another aspect of the situation that didn't make sense was that Tep and Luth had been left alive. The smart thing to do would have been to kill the two men. That way Amelia's disappearance would have been a mystery. The scenario most people would have believed was that the caravan had somehow gotten lost and the men and camels died. That Amelia would not be found could easily be explained. It would be presumed that she'd wandered away from the men, and that her body was buried by the windblown sand.

By allowing Tep and Luth to live, the bandits had left witnesses to their act. Then again, if Harad had not been in the desert looking for them, the two men would probably not have survived. They were beaten and on foot, without water. Another day of walking in the hot sun would probably have finished them off.

Harad was still running through the possibilities in his mind as he entered Dukhan Enterprises. He went straight up to his office and was greeted by a somewhat irritated Tut. The black cat demanded some delicacies, which Harad gave him as he continued to try to think through the events just past.

Harad's thoughts turned to Amelia and what she might be experiencing. He paced his office and thought about the quickest way to find her. The idea of her being looked upon or even touched as some form of human chattel made his body tense with anger. Twined through the anger was deep concern. She thought she was tough, but such an experience could devastate even the strongest woman. He stilled as he realized Amelia was not just his responsibility. He cared for her.

It wasn't only her beauty, but her spirit. She attacked life, taking no prisoners and giving no quarter. She decided what she wanted and then she went after it. Harad had thought Amelia was everything he didn't like in a woman, but now he realized those were qualities that he admired. And he had not often seen them in a woman.

Beneath the tough exterior, though, he sensed that Amelia had the heart of an eagle. Once she loved, she would love true and long. She was proud and free, soaring through life, but she had the trait of loyalty. Once she made her choice of a man, she would love him relentlessly. That she might not be allowed to make that choice freely was almost more than Harad could endure.

He had to find her and bring her back.

Calling the authorities was an option, but one Harad hesitated using. If things became too hot for the bandits, it was possible they would simply kill Amelia and leave her body in the sand. Though he could have used the professional help of the local authorities, Harad could not risk Amelia's safety. The best plan would be one that was low key.

The first step was to figure out who had taken Amelia. There were known bands of thieves and thugs who preyed upon travelers in the desert. Much like the old seagoing days of the pirates, when the skull and crossbones flew on ships that belonged to legendary cutthroats, there were well-known bandits in the desert.

Harad knew of two such men. Abdul the Terrible, so named because of the stories that circulated about his propensity to threaten to chop rich travelers to obtain their rings. Abdul terrified his ''guests'' with talk, not action. And there was Fayad Rama, who was said to maintain a band of at least fifty thieves in the middle of the Libyan Desert.

Harad had met Fayad once when he was a little boy. His mother had taken him when she went to speak with the pirate. Aleta Dukhan had actually hired Fayad to attack a caravan of archeologists who were getting a little too close to the lost City of Con.

The raid, though bloodless, had sent the scientists scuttling back to the safety of their respective countries. Aleta had been more than pleased with Fayad.

It was at least a place to start.

Harad was reaching for the telephone to make arrangements for his trip, when it rang. He picked it up, surprised to hear Dr. Kaffar Mosheen introducing himself.

''Have you found Amelia yet?'' the doctor asked. ''She hasn't answered her telephone messages all day. I was hoping you might have had better luck searching for her.''

Harad hesitated. He had to find out exactly what was happening with the doctor. ''I'm afraid Amelia has gone into the desert for several days,'' he said carefully. ''I tired to stop her, but I was too late. She was already gone. "What, exactly is wrong?" Harad pressed.

"What is your relationship to Miss Corbet?" the doctor asked unexpectedly.

"I'm her friend."

"I'm not at liberty to discuss her medical condition with *a friend*. But I will tell you that her condition may be far more serious than I at first knew. If you have any idea where she is, you must find her and convince her to return to the hospital here."

Harad kept rigid control of his voice—and his worries. "I'm sure Amelia will be in touch with you as soon as she returns to Alexandria."

"See that she does, Mr. Dukhan. I repeat, this is a very serious medical condition."

AMELIA LIFTED her chin and drank from the water bottle that her captor held to her mouth. He would not untie her hands, and now he was pretending that he didn't understand English. She wanted to spit at the men, to call them names and rail against the way they ignored her. She was tethered like one of the camels, and the idea that this might be her future treatment almost made her despair.

She was fighting back tears when the wicker basket on one of the camels popped open and the black cat leaped to the sand. He slithered between the camels' legs and watched the two bandits.

Amelia knew how desperate she was when she began to hope that the cat was some kind of miracle-working creature.

He was her only hope.

And Harad.

He'd made the arrangements for her trip. Surely, if Tep and Luth made it back to civilization, they would call him. He would hunt for her, and he would notify the authorities. Once her company knew she was missing and in danger, they would also begin to apply pressure, not to mention what her parents would do. Wealthy and influential, her parents would pressure Washington to pressure Cairo. Before long, there would be troops searching for her.

She held on to that thought as she forced back tears. Out of the corner of her eye she saw the cat scurry toward her.

Darting from the camels to the horses and finally to her, Familiar rushed to her back. She almost gasped when she felt something tickle her wrists before she figured out it was the cat's whiskers. He was using his mouth to try to loosen the bonds that held her.

"Holy cow," she whispered aloud. "You *are* trying to help me. Mauve and Harad weren't exaggerating."

The intensity of the work behind her hands increased. Amelia kept perfectly still, her gaze now on the two men who were talking quietly between themselves. The cat was still working on her when one of them stood up and walked toward her. The look on his face made her heart nearly stop.

"My friend thinks we should taste the fruits of the desert," he said slowly.

"Touch me and you will die." Amelia knew that

she ran the risk of annoying the man, but she didn't care. She wasn't going to beg and plead. And if he did touch her, she would make certain that he paid dearly for it.

"You are like a wild horse," he said, laughing. "You're wild, untamed. You'll soon learn the ways of survival."

"If you so much as touch my hair, I'll tell the man who buys me. I'll tell him everything you did to me. What will he do to you then? What will he think when he realizes you're selling him something you've used and discarded?"

Hidden by her back, Familiar was still furiously working at her bonds. She felt them loosen slightly, but she knew that even if the ropes fell away, she wasn't in a position to save herself.

The man grasped her arm and pulled her to her feet. Without another word he lifted her back onto the horse.

"It's time to go," he said, motioning his friend to prepare to ride.

Chapter Six

Amelia should be able to work her bonds free. She has to act fast, though. The very best she can hope for is a few minutes' lead. I'm not certain that's enough, and I don't know where she'll go if she does make a break for it. The desert can be more deadly than her captors. At least she'll have a chance to escape, should those men threaten her again. I, on the other hand, will be in serious trouble.

The best I can do is not draw attention to myself, so it's back into the basket for the moment. The captors are acting frantic. I get the sense that we're not far from wherever these men are taking us. All day I've been dreading the moment when we arrived at their camp, but I see some advantages.

Perhaps in the confusion of a camp, Amelia can sneak away and give herself the advantages of lead time and darkness to cover her tracks. I can figure out a way to get back to Alexandria. Based on Amelia's prior comments, I don't expect her to even give me a passing thought. I'm on my own.

So far, the men know that I'm in the basket, and

they seem unconcerned with a cat. I only hope they don't focus on Amelia again. She averted trouble once, but I doubt the same threat will work again. Our best tactic right now is to keep moving. And that's exactly what we're about to do.

All I can say is that I'll never complain about a horse again. This camel is about to kill me. I've been knocked from one side of the basket to the other. And I have excellent balance. Thank goodness the bandits put Amelia on a horse. Olli was about to beat her bottom to death.

The only good thing about my mode of transportation is this basket. The wicker provides a little shade from the sun. But soon night will be here. That means more problems for Amelia, I'm afraid. If we aren't at some settlement where these two men will be held in check by a leader, things could get mighty dicey.

"Ye-haa, camel. Get moving!"

HER TEETH HAD stopped chattering, but Amelia was still slightly queasy—and completely furious with herself. Her reaction to the guard's threat had been gut-churning fear. She'd managed to hide it behind an act of bravado, but she couldn't deny it to herself. Great! Extreme cowardice was exactly the emotion she didn't need.

All of her life she'd lived with the notion that if anyone ever physically threatened her, she'd be able to react in a calm, rational way. In business meetings she was cool, calm and deadly. She'd been known to smile at her enemies as she fiscally eviscerated them.

Not once had she felt even a flutter of fear. But looking into the eyes of the desert man who'd captured her, she'd seen a ruthlessness that left her knees weak. Instead of focusing on the fear, she had to keep her mind set on escape.

As her horse moved into an easy canter, she felt her body relax. As long as she was on the horse, she was safe. As much as she'd dreaded being taken to a settlement, she now felt that she'd be safer there than alone on the desert with the two men at night.

Gradually, her fear passed, and Amelia concentrated on devising a plan of escape. One of the men rode in front of her on the second horse. The other man followed behind the camels on Olli. Since she was in the middle, she didn't have much of a chance at making a break for it, but she was alert to any possibility.

Surreptitiously, she worked at her bonds. The cat had done a good job of loosening the knots, and she flexed her wrists and wiggled her hands until she felt certain she could slip out of the ropes.

With her hands freed, she could steer the horse. But in which direction? They were headed east, but where was Alexandria? To the north? Was there a closer settlement where she could seek aid?

She tried to visualize the map that Tep had shown her before they started out, but even though she knew where the dots of civilization showed on the map, it was vastly different from the reality of the desert. There wasn't a tree or sign or house or building or crack in the pavement that she could use for a landmark. There was only the sand, rolling dunes of it that burned golden and beautiful in the sunlight.

It would be an easy place to get lost and die.

Amelia tried not to think such morbid things. She glanced behind her at the camel that carried the wicker basket. The cat was peeping out, watching her.

Familiar. He'd come to her aid. When she did make her break for freedom, she couldn't leave the cat behind. He was a fellow American, she remembered Harad saying. Somewhere, his owners were looking for him. The two of them would safely make an escape.

The small caravan rode up another endless dune. As they crested the top, Amelia caught her breath. In the small valley below them was a lush green settlement. Tents billowed in the desert breeze, and palm trees offered shade.

"Oasis," she said, fully realizing the power of that word. It was magic, a place of water and green in the middle of sand and sun.

Horses and sheep grazed beside the tents, and young children ran and played, just as they would in any traditional village. The difference was the tents. They lent an air of impermanence to the entire scene. The nomadic tribes could be firmly encamped one moment, gone the next.

Amelia felt completely disconnected from her past life. She'd stepped into a world so very different from her own that comparisons were ineffective.

"Our leader will determine your fate," one of her captors said as he rode back to look at her.

He spurred his horse forward and began to gallop down the dune toward the settlement. The horses in the settlement noticed his arrival first, letting out a series of whinnies. The children picked up the hue and cry, followed by the women, and last of all the men. They came out of the tents fully armed.

Amelia felt as if she'd been physically touched as the gazes of the men shifted up to stare at her. Chills shook her, making even her fevered and sunburned face go cold. This wasn't good. It wasn't good at all.

Her captor signaled to the second man, who'd remained behind her on one of the camels.

"Ride!" he ordered Amelia.

Though her hands were nearly free, she had no option but to obey. To make a break for freedom now would be foolish. Taking a deep breath, she nudged her mare forward with her knees. She had never known such fear, and she had never been more determined not to show it.

HARAD LOOKED around him, at last satisfied with his preparations. He'd carefully studied the old desert maps prepared by his father. Suleman Dukhan had been a man of science. His love for Aleta, heir to the throne of Con, had been a stormy affair that had given him two sons and a wife who was a ruler not a partner. Though Suleman had left his wife and sons, he had given both boys a love of the stars and the laws of nature.

One of the most valuable things he'd left behind, right at this moment, were his maps. Suleman Dukhan had painstakingly documented every oasis in the entire Sahara Desert. Even the ones that were said to vanish during certain seasons. Even the ones that no one else could seem to find in the shifting sands.

Harad had determined that he had only one route open to him. If Amelia was being held captive by nomads who dealt in white slavery, he might be able to successfully trade with them. He might be able to get Amelia back with the loss of only money. If there was another, more civilized way, he didn't have time to think of it.

With her rescue and return to medical attention in mind, he'd pinpointed the most likely area of the desert that the nomads might be. Most of his youth had been spent as a nomad. He knew the things he'd need for survival, and he'd gathered them up.

Now he stood beside Pooldar and two packhorses, both loaded with supplies and the jewels and cash that he planned to use to buy Amelia's freedom. Few crooks could pass up ready cash. And just to be on the safe side, he'd also packed an automatic pistol and the knife that he was highly trained in using.

The flowing cotton of the robe he wore brushed over his legs, and though he was forty he felt again like a young man. It had been five years since he'd worn the traditional desert garb. Five years of suits and ties. The robes gave him a sense of freedom that he'd forgotten. As he walked toward Pooldar, he felt as if he'd stepped out of someone else's skin and returned to his own.

He knew then the power of the past. Though he'd

made a choice to put the desert behind him, it wasn't as easily done as he had thought. It was always there, just beneath the surface, ready to pull him back with a sensation or a memory. To his surprise, he found that his resistance was almost nonexistent. Perhaps it was time for him to reexplore the way of life that had been his childhood.

He was actually looking forward to riding Pooldar into the desert. It had been far too long since he'd sampled a way of life he'd thought was far behind him. The added incentive was Amelia. And the danger. Life as a businessman held many dangers. There was the risk of capital, the potential for disaster. But it was only financial ruin. As he checked the packs on the horses one more time, he realized that facing physical danger was far more exciting.

Mounting Pooldar, he picked up the leads for the two packhorses and set out into the waning afternoon. Traveling at night in the desert could be disorienting, but he knew the constellations and how to navigate by them. His father had often said that the desert was no different than the sea. Good navigational skills could help a man master both forms of nature.

Harad might have waited for a new day, but there wasn't enough time. Amelia was in danger on two fronts—medically, and from her captors. Every hour she remained in the hands of the traders put her that much closer to injury. His fondest hope was that she was smart enough not to antagonize her captors. Knowing Amelia's personality, though, he somehow thought that was a foolish hope. She could irritate the whiskers off a camel.

"Come on, Pooldar," he whispered to the horse as soon as they stepped into the desert. "Run like the wind."

AMELIA TRIED TO make herself small as she was pulled from the horse and thrust into the middle of a crowd of gawking people. A hand reached out and touched her hair. Her first instinct was to pull away, but she made herself stand firm. She lifted her chin and turned to stare at the woman who'd touched her.

Soft green eyes looked into her own.

"So this is the prize we were told about," a heavyset man said in English as he came forward. He nodded as he walked around Amelia. "Yes, it is as he promised."

It was on the tip of Amelia's tongue to demand who had promised what, but she felt a slight pressure on her arm. The green-eyed woman pressed a finger into her biceps. Her eyes warned Amelia to remain quiet.

"She'll bring a good price," one of her captors said as another man slapped him on the back.

The heavyset man, obviously the leader, spoke again in a language she couldn't understand. But when she felt hands grasp her arms and begin to push her in the direction of a tent, she knew what had been said. She'd been sent to another form of prison, this one made of cotton. As she stood in the tent opening, she felt the bonds on her hands loosened. The green-eyed woman turned Amelia to stare into her eyes.

"You could have freed your hands," the woman said.

"And gone where?" Amelia answered.

The woman nodded. "I'll see to some refreshments for you." She was gone in a swirl of flowing material.

Amelia found herself inside a tent that was already furnished with pillows and hangings. It was surprisingly comfortable looking. The sand was covered with a thick wool carpet that was so beautiful she knelt down and ran her fingers over it. In the fairy tales she'd read, such a carpet would be able to fly. In the States, such a rug would fetch a handsome price.

The pillows that made up the bed were lush and covered in a dark tapestry. She sank down in them and realized that her legs were throbbing. Horseback riding was one sport that required practice and constancy to avoid soreness. What she needed was a long, hot soak.

As if someone had read her thoughts, the flap of the tent opened and the green-eyed woman returned. Behind her two men brought in a tub. Several women with heated containers of water followed.

The green-eyed woman signaled them to pour the water into the tub and then waved them all out.

"Refresh yourself," she said. "You will be undisturbed for now. Abdul will wish to speak with you later."

She started to leave, but Amelia jumped up and

caught her arm. ''Tell them my parents will pay a big ransom.''

A trace of a smile touched the woman's lips. ''It would be simpler to give them what they really want,'' she said.

''What they really want?'' Amelia repeated the phrase. ''What would that be?''

''They call me Ko,'' the woman said. ''It's a name of affection for someone who is not right in the head. I was brought here, like you, and I chose to stay.''

''Look, my folks will pay them whatever they want. I just want to get out of here, get on a plane and get to Paris where I can finish my business. I won't tell anyone about this. The authorities won't be contacted. You have my word.''

The woman looked at her steadily. ''You don't understand what's going on, do you?''

''I was abducted. My guides were beaten and left for dead. I understand that laws have been broken by the two men who kidnapped me.''

''Abdul and his men don't give the laws of the city a lot of regard,'' she said. ''Here, it is the law of the sand that dictates life and death. By that law, you are bounty.''

''I'm a human being, an American citizen, a business—''

''You are a woman, and you've been brought from the desert. Like a wild horse, you belong to the man who caught you.'' Ko made a wry face. ''It's the law of the desert.''

''I'll show them the law of the desert. I'll—''

"Whatever else you do, don't threaten Abdul or his men. I know the world you come from. You may expect at least a nod toward equality. Don't. Never forget that in the eyes of the men, you are a creature without rights. There is one thing I can tell you. You will do as they say. It's easiest to do it willingly."

Amelia sensed that Ko was trying to help her, but the advice she was handing out was bitter medicine. "You said you chose to stay here. Why?"

Ko smiled. "You'll find out soon enough. Your water grows cold. Bathe and rest. Tonight you will have a chance to barter for your freedom. You must be alert, and you must be entertaining. The weapon you must use is charm. Use it wisely."

Ko walked out of the tent and left Amelia with her thoughts. She went to the tub, contemplating turning it over and letting the water ruin the carpet and pillows. It would be her first act of defiance.

She dipped her hand into the water and realized that a hot bath would do her more good than destruction of her accommodations. Quickly she disrobed and stepped into the water. With a loud sigh she sank down, letting the hot water rise over her body. It was lightly scented and oiled. Soap and a cloth had been provided, as well as a big towel.

When the water had grown cool, she stepped out and dried. To her surprise, a robe was beneath the towel. Her own clothes were dirty, and she slipped the robe over her head. The feel of it was slightly unsettling. It was almost like wearing nothing at all.

She couldn't be certain, but the fabric seemed flimsier than the robes the men wore. And it hugged her curves, revealing almost as much as if she wore nothing.

Amelia decided to wear it until she was summoned before the leader. Then she would need her own clothes.

Her own clothes. Odd how something like clothes gave her such a sense of identity. Wearing the robe, she felt as if she'd lost another tie with her real life.

What was Ko's story? She wasn't born in the Bedouin tribe. She was European. Amelia was sure of that. Yet she'd chosen to live in a community where women had few rights. Why? Amelia intended to find out—if she stayed around long enough.

She heard a scratching at the tent and hurried to the back side. A black paw shot through the sand and under the tent. In a moment, Familiar had dug a hole big enough to slide his entire body through.

He stopped as he looked up at her.

"Me-ow!"

As incredible as it was, Amelia felt a blush creeping over her face. It was as if the cat was complimenting her on the robe. Ridiculous, but the way he was staring at her made her feel self-conscious in the clinging folds of apricot material.

Amelia went to the pillows and sank into them. The cat followed, hopping onto her lap. Amelia began to stroke the cat's soft fur. It was strange, but she derived a sense of comfort from the black feline. He was extraordinary, no doubt about that. But he made her feel as if she had an ally.

"I have to get out of here tonight," she said.

"Meow," the cat agreed, nodding his head.

"Once the camp is asleep, I'll try to find my little mare. I think I can ride her without a saddle. I want you to come with us."

"Meow!" The cat nodded again.

"That's the plan." She knew it was foolishly simple, and completely without detail. But there was no way to plan better. She hadn't been allowed to look around the settlement. She didn't know the routine of the camp. She would be flying by the seat of her pants. She took a deep breath and bent down to brush a kiss on Familiar's head.

"I'm smarter than all of these men put together," she whispered. "I just have to remember that."

The cat grew still in her lap, and she felt her body tense in response. She looked up to find one of the men who'd kidnapped her standing in the open tent flap, staring at her with what could only be described as a look of hunger.

"Abdul will see you now."

Chapter Seven

Pooldar was blowing hard when Harad finally reined him in and allowed him to stop on the crest of a steep dune. The packhorses were equally winded, and Harad, too, was breathing hard. Above them a million stars winked and twinkled.

It was a beautiful night with fingers of cold that touched Harad's exposed face and hands. The desert was an exotic mixture of contrasts. The almost unbearable heat of the day gave way to a cold that could be bone chilling once the sun had slipped beyond the horizon. Seasoned desert travelers knew the fluctuations of temperature and prepared for them. Harad wrapped the long folds of his headdress around his lower face and neck. The gear of the Bedouin was designed to serve a purpose. The long folds of material were effective against the cold and, more importantly, they blocked blowing sand during a storm.

There was no need to consult the map that he carried. He'd memorized each tiny detail. By his best calculations, he was only an hour or so from the oasis that he'd decided was the most likely spot for the kidnappers to be camped.

Oasis Lulal. It was a place with a reputation for vanishing and therefore was seldom used by the guides who took tourists into the desert. But it was a haven for the true desert dwellers. Since it was seldom used, it was safe. Harad's people had used the oasis in the past as a camp that was close to Alexandria and not too far from Cairo. In recent years, though, the Oasis Lulal had changed. The raiders and thieves who preyed upon travelers found it a convenient hideout.

Harad wondered about the true nature of the oasis. His father had taught him respect for science not superstition. He'd never failed to find the Oasis Lulal when he sought it, but there were many tales of travelers who'd died while searching for the necessary water that the oasis offered.

Legends had grown up about it. The stories said that it could be found only by the true Bedouins, the tribes of the desert who lived on the dunes.

It was a romantic notion, but one that Harad didn't believe. More than likely, those who'd gotten lost had not been good navigators or had been outfitted with improper maps. An oasis simply couldn't disappear or hide itself on a whim.

If it could, Harad knew he was in serious trouble. After the hard ride, his animals were weary and needed rest and water. The accuracy of his calculations was vital. Pooldar and the packhorses could not survive if he missed the target. Without the horses, he would not live.

The two pack animals stood with their heads down, resting. Pooldar was too proud to let his head droop. Harad patted the stallion's neck. The horse had spirit. He was tireless, and he would give everything that Harad asked.

Tightening his legs on the stallion, Harad asked for more. He had to find Amelia. And he had to do it soon. The American woman had to be found and brought back to Alexandria safely.

Although his biggest concern was for Amelia's personal safety, Harad knew a lot more was riding on this than just that. In the long hours of crossing the desert, he'd come to realize that Amelia's abduction could do far more to jeopardize the way of life of the nomadic tribes than Beth's work ever could. By revealing the secrets of Con, Beth could destroy his people and their chosen life. If Amelia was hurt in any way, the attention of the world would focus on the desert people—all of them. They would all be tarred with the same brush. They would be labeled barbarians, and their way of life viewed as unsavory.

It was true that young women disappeared from every city in the world. Bad things happened, and it was unfortunate. But Amelia was an international businesswoman. Her company and her family would make this an international issue.

As well they should.

But a lot of innocent people would suffer for the sins of a few.

Harad leaned back in the saddle as Pooldar skittered down the steep slope of the dune. The horse was almost sitting down as he slipped in the deep sand, scurrying toward the bottom of the incline. Harad gave him his head and did all he could to keep the pack animals on a loose lead so that they, too, could find their balance and negotiate the dune without his interference.

Amelia.

Harad's gut clenched. Mosheen's call flashed through his mind, one more reason he must rescue Amelia quickly. He debated telling her when they finally met, and decided not to. She had undoubtedly been through enough for the time being. He would make it in time, and pray he could get her back before she was hurt in any way.

He must.

AMELIA STOPPED in her tracks. The men were seated on pillows on the ground around a fire. She'd been so hastily pulled from her tent that she hadn't had a chance to change back into her own clothes, and the flowing apricot robe she wore made her feel more naked than clothed. The fabric covered her from head to toe, but it whispered sensually across her skin with each step she took. That sensation was an alarm bell in her mind.

Walking to stand in front of the men, she held herself perfectly still.

"Ko says that your family will pay a large ransom for you," Abdul said without preamble.

"Name your price. They will pay it, but only as long as I'm not hurt in any way." She put extra emphasis on the last three words.

Abdul laughed. "I see." He leaned over and whispered with another man, who joined in his laughter.

Amelia clenched her hands into fists. Her first impulse was to take the two steps forward and kick Abdul right in the face. It would be one of the most satisfying things she'd ever done—and probably one of the most costly. Like it or not, she was at this man's mercy, and she knew better than to do something that might jeopardize his decision.

"How much will they pay?"

She hadn't thought of a figure. What would these people think of as a lot of money?

"Ten thousand dollars." She said it clearly.

Abdul laughed. "We were paid twice that to find you," he said, punching the man beside him in the ribs. He repeated everything in his language and all the men began to laugh.

"How much do you want?" Amelia asked. She was burning to know who had paid money to have her found. Something about this entire mess wasn't right. How had her two captors known where to find her? How had they known she would have only Tep and Luth with her? Something was very wrong, and the finger of suspicion pointed straight at Harad. If she could figure it out, she would also be able to determine the degree of her danger. She had to keep her wits about her, her ears open and her temper under control. That was the route to survival.

The black cat walked up to the fire and sat down, not fifteen yards from the men. Several turned to look at him, but no one made a move toward him. Amelia wondered if they thought he was one of the cats in the settlement. It was amazing that an entire village, complete with horses, camels, sheep, children and cats could pack up and move, but she knew they could. If she didn't play her cards right, she would be moving right along with them.

"Could your family give us half a million American dollars?"

Amelia bit back the gasp that almost escaped her. "That's a large amount of money," she said carefully. "It would take time." She started to explain that assets would have to be sold, accounts liquidated and rearranged. "That amount would also draw the attention of the American government."

"Why would the government care about such things?" Abdul asked with a crafty note in his voice. "If your parents are as wealthy as you say, why would the government know or care what they did with their money?"

Amelia took a breath. How to explain to a bandit about the IRS? "The government keeps an eye on large transactions because in America there's often a tax. They care because they want to be sure they get their portion." She cut him off before he could ask. "There's no way to hide this. The government will know. But a more reasonable amount could be managed. And very quickly."

Interest lit his eyes, and she thought she might be

making progress. One of the men leaned over and whispered in his ear.

"Then we shall have to keep you until your family pays all of it in small amounts," Abdul said.

"That could take months!" Amelia regretted her outburst as soon as the words were out of her mouth. Abdul was openly laughing at her, and the other men grinned.

"You are strong and healthy. You'll make someone a good wife until then," Abdul said.

"I'll be no man's wife!" Amelia couldn't help herself. The situation was intolerable. She'd never had to have a cup of coffee with a man she didn't choose to be with. The idea that Abdul could so casually determine a husband for her was infuriating.

Abdul rose gracefully to his feet for such a heavy-set man. "You will do as I say. Do not forget that, Amelia Corbet. The life here can be easy or hard, as you choose. Now return to your tent while we decide your fate."

"But—"

She felt biting fingers in her arm and turned to see Ko's green eyes blazing into her. Ko jerked her arm and pushed her back the way she'd come.

"Shut up and move," Ko warned her.

Amelia felt her face burn with fury, but she walked in the direction Ko shoved her. When they were safely out of earshot of the men, Amelia whirled around.

"Who do they think they are? They can't do this. I won't have it."

Ko took a deep breath. "The first thing you have to learn is that you aren't queen here. The rules are very different. If you aren't careful, though, you're going to end up in big trouble."

"I'm already in big trouble. He's going to marry me off to one of those barbarians until my folks can raise half a million dollars. You know, the best thing that could happen would be for my family to contact the president. Then Abdul the Awful would see what happens when an American citizen is taken against her will."

They were at the tent and Ko lifted the flap, ushering Amelia inside. When they were face-to-face in the tent lighted by a lantern, Ko lightly touched Amelia's face, forcing Amelia's gaze to hers.

"First of all, I think Abdul was kidding with you. Half a million is not even reasonable, and he knows it. The ten thousand you mentioned is more the going price for a kidnap victim. Second of all, there's more to this than just a kidnapping for ransom."

"They said they were going to sell me," Amelia said, still angry, but beginning to be calmed by Ko's reasonable approach.

"It's possible, but to be honest, you're a little old for that."

"Old! I'm only thirty-three!"

Ko laughed. "My, vanity overrules self-preservation."

Amelia finally saw the humor of it and shook her head with a rueful smile. "That was ridiculous."

"Look, I don't think you're in any danger for the

moment. My suggestion is that you get some rest and try to find something else to wear tomorrow.'' She gave the robe a long look. ''I'll see what I can find out.''

''Why are you doing this?''

Ko looked as if she might not answer. ''In many ways, Abdul is like a child. He rules his tribe, but he has no idea about the rest of the world. I happen to believe you when you say your family will call the United States president. I know that if that should happen, it is possible that the army will come into the desert to search for you. If that happens, no one will be overly concerned about what happens to us.'' She hesitated. ''I love a man of this tribe. I've come to love his people as my family. I don't want to see them destroyed by Abdul's foolish schemes.''

''How did you get here?'' Amelia asked, for once forgetting her own predicament. She was fascinated by Ko.

''A story for another time,'' the woman said.

''Can you tell me where you're from?'' Amelia pressed.

''Edinburgh. And that's the last bit of information you'll get tonight. Sleep. You may need all of your strength tomorrow. I had your things brought to the tent.''

Ko gestured to where Amelia's pack and purse sat on the rug, then slipped through the tent flap.

Amelia gave it ten minutes, then went to the flap, easing it open. A tall silhouette stepped in front of her, blocking her path.

With a snort of disgust, Amelia turned around and went to the pillows where she flopped down. She'd expected there to be a guard on her doorway—if you could call a tent flap a doorway. Still, it made her angry. Even if they'd given her her things, There was no room for doubt that she was a prisoner.

HARAD TOPPED the dune and halted, letting the relief sweep through him as he gazed down on the village of tents. Oasis Lulal was playing host to someone, and Harad felt his hopes rise. It was reasonable to believe he'd found the place where Amelia was being held.

Now he had to make sure his strategy worked.

He went over all the things that might give him away, and he concluded that only Amelia's reaction would be a problem. If she indicated in any way that she knew him, they would both be in grave danger.

Easing Pooldar forward, he led the packhorses toward the oasis. Desert etiquette would demand that he be received with courtesy and hospitality. His horses would be watered and fed, as would he. That much he knew.

The alert went up as soon as the perimeter guard saw him. Some would have thought it the cry of a hawk, but Harad knew it for what it was—a signal to the settlement that a stranger was approaching. The men at the oasis would be reaching for their weapons.

He rode slowly forward, giving everyone time to see that he was a solitary man without weapons. Or at least weapons they could see. He was not a fool.

One semiautomatic pistol would be virtually useless against a village, but he had it nonetheless. He hoped he never had to draw it.

He halted on the edge of the settlement, sitting quietly as several men came up to him, walked around his animals and finally returned to face him.

"What is your business here?" they asked.

"I'm a traveler," he said, waiting a beat. "A traveler on a quest for a very special prize." He made a movement with his hand that drew the men's attention to the big ruby that he'd deliberately slid onto his finger. A heavy gold bracelet slipped down his wrist. He'd purchased both pieces of jewelry for this occasion.

He had the guard's interest.

"I've heard that there are people in the desert who sometimes *find* this type of treasure."

"What type of treasure do you seek?" The man's gaze was on the ruby that winked red, reflecting the leaping flames of a nearby fire.

"Something gold, but silkier than gold. Something bluer than sapphires. Something soft and warm, to ease the cold of desert nights." He waited, watching the look that passed among the men. They knew exactly what he was talking about, and they had Amelia. "I know that such a treasure is difficult to find. I expect to pay a handsome price for such a thing, if I should be lucky enough to find someone willing to trade."

"There is no such treasure in this camp," one of the men said gruffly.

"I have been searching for this for many months." Harad shrugged. "I will continue tomorrow."

A hand grasped Pooldar's reins, and Harad's initial reaction was to spin the horse away. But he allowed the man to lead him into the settlement. Someone had taken the packhorses from him.

"I'm grateful for your hospitality," Harad said, as if there was no other possible action that could be taken against him. "My horses are weary."

"This is a fine animal," the guard said, eyeing Pooldar.

"Yes, he is."

"He would improve the quality of our herd," the man continued.

"He is a superior stallion," Harad agreed.

"Our leader, Abdul, will be very interested in seeing him."

"I would be delighted to talk with Abdul," Harad said.

The man indicated that Pooldar and the other horses would be watered and fed. Harad's packs were lifted from the animals and taken into the tent that the guard was now indicating for Harad to enter. "Abdul will send for you."

Harad dismounted and watched as Pooldar was led away. He'd never anticipated that his horse would be of more interest than jewels, but he shouldn't have been surprised. His younger brother had been establishing a breeding program for the past five years. He'd talked endlessly of the future of the nomadic tribes and horses. Harad knew for once he should have been paying a lot more attention to Omar and his plans.

He entered the tent, freshened up with water from the bowl left for him and began searching through his saddlebag for the things he would need.

A small movement in the tent made him stop. He'd assumed it was empty. A sigh of relief escaped him as the black cat jumped onto a pillow. Once again, Familiar had appeared where least expected. There was no doubt now that Amelia was here.

He'd just finished putting together his gift offering when someone came to escort him to meet Abdul. Harad clutched the felt bag in his hand as he walked to a brightly burning fire. Several men sat around it, and Harad made the bows of respect to all of them. He knew Abdul by his position of authority in the center of the group. He handed him the felt bag.

"A small gift of my thanks for your hospitality," he said.

Abdul opened the bag, shaking out a handsome wristwatch. It was expensive, and Harad was glad it was when he saw the appreciative smile on Abdul's face.

"My men tell me you are searching for a special treasure," Abdul said.

"Yes. I fear I must keep looking, though."

"You have had no success?" Abdul asked.

"One or two offers, but the treasure was not special enough. I fear I'm a man with discriminating taste. I want fire and spirit, like my horse."

Abdul chuckled. "Perhaps we may be able to help

each other,'' he said. ''There is such a woman here. She is not here willingly, and I fear to keep her. She makes threats that trouble my advisers.''

''What kind of threats can a woman make that troubles a man?'' Harad asked, knowing that he was stepping on Abdul's toes.

''Threats about foreign governments. The U.S. government. This woman is an American, and it seems her family has some influence in the area of politics.''

''Women disappear all the time. Was she in Cairo?'' he asked.

''On the desert,'' Abdul answered.

''Even better. She is lost, another victim of the sun.'' He shrugged. ''Terrible things happen to unwary travelers.''

Abdul grinned slowly. ''Yes, that's true. But I agreed to keep this woman for a friend. Now I think he has asked too much of me.''

''You would be willing for me to take her off your hands?'' Harad asked. So, Amelia had been threatening and running her mouth. She'd softened the road for him.

''For a price,'' Abdul asserted quickly. ''She's valuable. A magnificent woman, if a little too filled with talk.''

''What of your friend?'' Harad asked. He had to find out more about this mysterious person.

Abdul shrugged. ''He paid for us to take her. He said we were to keep her for several days. Now, it seems, it would be best for my people if she left us. She should depart as soon as possible."

Harad thought of an old saying about thieves and honor, but he only nodded. "Let me see this prize," he said.

"She needs some work on conducting herself properly," Abdul warned.

Harad smiled. "I would see her dance," he said. "Yes. Bring her here to me. I would see her dance."

He settled back, pulling the folds of his headdress up to cover his face as much as possible. Fireworks were imminent, and he hid his smile at the thought of what Amelia's reaction to a command performance would be.

There was every possibility that before the night was over, Abdul would pay him to take Amelia off his hands.

Chapter Eight

Harad has arrived, and just in the nick of time. But he's out there powwowing with the bigwigs of the settlement, and I somehow don't like that look of satisfaction on his face. He's up to something, and now isn't the time for fun and games. He'll learn that the hard way, I'm afraid. I know he has feelings for Amelia, even if he won't admit them to himself. To be honest, though, I can see where she brings out a man's worst qualities—meaning those that might take the tiniest bit of pleasure in seeing her in this predicament. After all, it is her stubbornness, orneriness and downright unwillingness to listen to reason that has brought her to this pass. Amen.

They're bringing Amelia forward again, and she's fighting like a wild animal. She should learn that it only gives them a sense of fun to play tug-of-war with her arms. Dang, she's hardheaded.

I wish Ko would come along and counsel Amelia. She seems to be the only person who can talk sense into Madame Taurus. I just hope that Amelia is paying enough attention to what's going on not to blow

Harad's cover. And I'm beginning to have some serious second thoughts about exactly what Harad's cover might be. It's interesting that they've chosen to converse mostly in English. A sign that even Abdul is not too eager for the rest of his tribe to know the details of what he's up to. That is a clue, but I'm just not certain to what.

Harad, though, has waded into treacherous waters. I heard enough of the conversation between him and Abdul to deduce that he might be trying to purchase Madame Taurus. All I can say is that either he's addicted to danger or he's a total fool. Amelia will annihilate him, and I don't blame her. She won't care that he's trying to get her out of a pinch. The idea that he negotiated a price for her will send her into a fit.

They've taken Amelia into another tent. Uh-oh. They're taking her robe and putting some "I Dream of Jeannie" costume on her. She's spitting like a cat in a tub of water. And cursing! I'm surprised that someone as refined as Amelia knows some of those words. Boy! Just goes to show you that appearances can be deceiving.

Some strange music is starting up in the background. A woman is putting something on Amelia's fingers. They're like little brass cymbals. She's showing her how to click them together to make them ring in time to the music.

Now one of the women is grasping Amelia's hips and showing her how to move them to the music. Hmm. She's got a better sense of rhythm than I would have thought. And she can rotate those hips. Reminds me of one of my favorite lines from a Sam Spade mystery—something about her hips waving hello. Gotta love that image.

My goodness, the total effect of Amelia would make Barbara Eden stay in her genie bottle. She is a knockout! Somehow, though, I don't see Amelia calling anyone master, though she does seem to have mastered this belly-dancing technique.

The women are clapping at Amelia, and she's starting to show off. I don't think that's smart, but how can I tell her that? Conveniently forgetting that she's a kidnapping victim, she's acting as if this is a big girls' pajama party. It only goes to show you that Amelia can't truly accept that she's in a pickle. She really believes that no one would dare to hurt her.

Well, here comes the spoiler to that fantasy. The man is dragging Amelia out of the hut and toward the fire. The music is louder here, and the women have followed. They're chattering and clapping.

They've brought Amelia to stand in front of the fire and left her. She is furious. Her chest is heaving up and down, and if she isn't careful she's going to fall out of that tiny little top. I wish I could warn her that all that heavy breathing is making the gold belt around her bare waist catch the firelight. Quite attractive, I must say, and every man sitting around the fire is fully aware of every single one of her assets.

Tall and slender, Amelia looks terrific in that getup. The skirt she's wearing is full, but it's split into several pieces so that each time she takes a step, her leg slips through the material. And what a set of gams! Believe me, there's not a man watching who hasn't noticed.

Abdul is commanding her to dance. I see the fire of rebellion in Amelia's eyes. She's going to refuse. This is not going to be a pretty sight, but at least she hasn't recognized Harad. Oh, this is going to be a long night. When I get home, I'm going to write a book.

AMELIA HEARD the women behind her clapping encouragement. She felt the eyes of everyone on her, but her attention was drawn to a man sitting beside Abdul. His face was concealed, but his dark eyes watched her with amusement.

In all of her life, Amelia had never been subjected to the role of toy. The idea that some arrogant man found her amusing made her want to fight.

"Dance!" Abdul commanded her again.

For a split second, Amelia remained frozen. Every fiber of her spirit told her to tell the chieftain to go straight to Hades. She'd dance when she felt like dancing and not before.

All of her life, she'd taken action and let others worry about the fallout, but this time the possibility of the consequences stopped her. Dancing was far preferable to some of the other things she might be ordered to do. She could refuse to dance, but ultimately she had no recourse.

At least not now. There would come a time when Abdul and his henchmen would pay dearly for this moment. She'd often been told that she needed to cultivate patience and compassion. Now was the time for patience.

From behind her she heard Ko's voice urging her to comply. "Dance for them, Amelia," Ko urged her. "Mesmerize them. It will be to your advantage."

Slowly Amelia began to move to the music. She kept her gaze above the heads of the men and danced. As a girl she'd had ballet, tap and modern-dance lessons. Though she'd loved the lessons and the sense of freedom that movement gave her, none of the practice seemed much use in this place. The strange, undulating music required a wilder, more spontaneous response.

Slowly she allowed her body to move to the beat. Her long hair, unbraided, swung around her face and shoulders. She made sure to keep as far away from the audience of men as possible. A rug had been placed on the sand, and her bare feet moved over it.

When she did finally look at the stranger, she saw that he was sitting forward. He whispered something to Abdul and pulled a ring off his finger and handed it to the leader.

More whispering ensued, and at last the music stopped. Amelia turned her back on the men and walked into the crowd of laughing women. No one tried to stop her, and she went to her tent.

She was both angry and exhilarated. She also knew that she had to find a way to escape. The little episode of dancing, though it had proven harmless so far, was enough to show her that she could not endure a lot more of taking orders. She thought of her life in Manhattan, where she charted her own destiny—and that of others—on an hourly basis. Growing up in a home where she'd been treated as an equal, she'd come to expect equality from everyone she met. She sat down on the pillows.

No, she didn't expect equality, she expected a lot more. She was crackerjack at her profession, and she had come to expect recognition for her talents and energy.

This world she'd stumbled into had no use for her public relations skills, her quick wit, her communication skills, her ability to wine and dine clients and convince them that Bretzel and Burke was the only agency that could handle their needs. She had been not only good at her job. She'd been the best. And she'd come to believe that she had value.

For a fleeting moment, she thought of her apartment and all the things her talent had brought her. The view was spectacular—the East River. Though she had several magnificent Persian carpets, they were laid on marble not sand. Her furnishings followed a theme of natural wood and white. It gave the apartment a feel of clean spaciousness. On one of Beth's rare visits, she'd tentatively offered that the effect of Amelia's decor was a little cold. Amelia hadn't thought so. It was perfect for her. Not a knickknack or gewgaw to clutter up the lines of the beautiful furnishings.

Amelia picked up her jeans and boots. It was time to get dressed and get the heck out of here. She'd come to the desert to find her sister, and all she'd done was get herself into a mess of trouble. Well, she was Amelia Corbet, high-powered executive of a firm with international offices. It was time she remembered that and quit fooling around.

The tent flap parted and Ko stepped inside. Her face was drawn into a frown.

"What is it?" Amelia asked.

"Abdul has made a deal. The stranger has purchased you," she said simply.

Amelia felt as if a fork of lightning had struck her. She could find no words.

"I was sent to prepare you to receive him." Ko looked at the floor as she spoke.

"Over my dead body," Amelia finally sputtered.

"He will be here any minute. You must reconcile yourself," Ko said. She shook her head. "I have never seen this happen. Abdul is a thief and kidnapper, but he has never traded in women."

"That makes me feel a lot better," Amelia fumed. She began pulling her jeans up under the flowing skirt of her dance costume. "I'm out of here and don't try to stop me."

"You won't get ten yards," Ko warned her, but she made no effort to stop Amelia.

"Help me," Amelia said.

Ko bit her lip. "There is nothing I can do. I would help you, but there's not a chance you can escape from the settlement." She came forward and grasped Amelia's hands. "Listen to me. If this man takes you away, he travels alone. You'll have a better chance of escaping when you are with him."

"What about tonight?" Amelia asked. "I won't do this."

Ko paced the room, her forehead creased with a frown. At last she stopped. "Then you must try to escape now. I'll go and saddle a horse for you. I'll put some food and water in a pack tied to the saddle."

Amelia grasped her hands. "Thank you, Ko. I'll always remember this."

"We must hurry. I'll—"

The tent flap opened and the stranger stepped into the tent. He looked at Ko. "Leave us," he said in a voice that expected obedience.

Ko leaned toward Amelia. "Remember, freedom is your goal. Do what you must." She stopped at the door of the tent and threw Amelia a look of sympathy before she ducked through the opening and into the night.

Amelia found herself alone with a man who had bought her like a horse. Her heart was pounding painfully in her chest. Never in a million years would she have ever predicted her life could have reached such a place.

HARAD KNEW the game was over. It was time to reveal his identity to Amelia, and Kaffar Mosheen's message had made it that much more important that they escape quickly. Yet the images of her dancing, backlit by the fire, played again and again in his mind. The flash of leg, the sway of her hips and the spun gold of her hair were erotic visions that tantalized Harad. She was the most extraordinarily sensual woman he'd ever seen. Her businesslike exterior was just a facade, but a very good one. He suspected that few men had truly seen through it to the woman.

He'd just paid a fortune for her. As the thought of his deal with Abdul crossed his mind, he smiled. Amelia was going to throw a conniption fit once she found out about it.

"Whatever you think you're doing, you won't live to lay a finger on me," Amelia asserted loudly.

"Hush," Harad whispered. He knew several of the men were lurking outside the tent to see how he would fare with the blond spitfire. Bets had been laid that she would inflict some sort of injury on him.

"You can't buy another human being," Amelia said, her voice growing louder.

"Be quiet," Harad said. "I can explain—"

"Explain nothing. What kind of man needs to buy a woman?" she asked. With each statement, she grew louder. "What's wrong with you that you can't get one willingly?"

Harad heard laughter outside the tent. If Amelia didn't quiet down, he would be forced to take an action that would silence her.

"Just calm down," he said, stepping toward her.

"Stay away!" Amelia picked up a glass and hurled it at him.

The attack was unexpected, and Harad diverted the glass with his hand. The contents splashed against the tent wall.

"Stop behaving like a spoiled brat," Harad said.

"I'll show you spoiled brat." Amelia picked up a tray of food and heaved it at him.

Harad easily ducked the food and stepped closer to her. "Amelia, stop it," he whispered.

"Get away from me!" She moved backward, her hands seeking another weapon. She found her boots and threw them, one after the other. The second one caught Harad on the temple.

Outside the tent, the men's laughter had grown louder. Amelia was creating quite a scene, and the longer it went on, the harder it would be for the two of them to eventually make an escape.

Without warning, Harad dived at her. He caught her against him and fell back onto the pillows with her beneath them. He realized his tactical mistake when he felt her kicking, gouging and clawing with all her might.

"Amelia," he whispered. "Stop this now. I'm here to help you." But he knew she was beyond listening. She was fighting for her life. Her slender body pressed against his, and the more she struggled to get away from him, the more she came into contact with his body.

Harad had no wish to restrain her, but he knew he had to capture her hands before she clawed his eyes out. He caught her wrists and pinned them above her head.

She lashed out with a knee, almost catching him in a very tender spot. He used his thigh to divert the thrust and then rested his weight across her. ''Amelia!''

She was so panicked, she didn't hear a thing he was saying. Reaching up, he tried to pull away the folds of material that covered his face. Before he could accomplish that, Amelia sank her teeth into his hand.

He bit back the yell, knowing that it would only bring others into the tent.

''Amelia!'' He could not risk yelling—any excuse would bring the men into the tent—so he was reduced to whispering harshly.

She only struggled harder, her blue eyes blazing with anger and fear.

He pinned her more firmly to the pillows, determined to hold her until she calmed enough to listen to him.

''You will die,'' she whispered harshly. ''You will regret the day you were born. You will suffer a million agonies.'' Her voice broke. ''You will be sorry for this for the rest of your life.'' She squinted her eyes shut and held her body rigid.

Harad saw the tears leak out from beneath her eyelids. His weight was crushing the air out of her lungs, and she'd quit fighting, but she was far from giving up. She might have to yield to his superior strength, but she would never willingly consent to his touch.

The tears were his undoing. If he'd ever thought he might enjoy playing this moment out—tormenting her with her position—he knew he was wrong. It was no pleasure to see such spirit being broken. ''Listen to me, Amelia,'' he whispered softly in her ear. ''It's Harad. I've come to help you.''

He felt her grow even stiffer, then relax.

''Harad?''

He lifted his face so that she could see his eyes. ''It's me. I'll let you go if you promise not to try and kill me.''

''Take that thing off your face.''

He wanted to smile at the tone of authority that had returned to her voice. She'd been on the verge of defeat, but as he suspected, it was only a temporary lull. He let her wrists go and rolled to the side, completely freeing her from his weight.

With a quick movement, he removed the headpiece.

''Har—''

He clamped a hand over her mouth. ''Hush. That's what I've been trying to tell you. They think I'm some kind of merchant. If they knew who I really was, they'd probably kill me.''

''We have to get out of here.'' Amelia sat up.

Her blond hair was tumbled down her back, and in the melee, the top of her costume had slipped down. Harad's gaze lingered on the full breasts that were almost free of the top.

Amelia stood up, adjusting her clothes. ''Hurry up, Harad, let's get out of here.''

He caught her wrist and pulled her to face him, more than a little amused at the flush on her face. ''It isn't that simple. We can leave in the morning, but not tonight.''

"Why not?"

"I have to pay Abdul the rest of what I owe him for you."

"Don't be absurd. You don't owe him a thing."

"That's your point of view." Whatever damage Amelia might have sustained viewing herself as chattel, she was quickly getting over it. She was back in command mode. Harad was hardly able to suppress his amusement. She had tremendous bounce-back.

"Why should we wait until morning? Just go pay him. Don't worry, we'll get the money back. I intend to report him to the authorities and I'll see him behind bars."

Harad's left eyebrow lifted. "I can't pay him. Yet. I have to assure myself that the merchandise is worth the purchase price."

That statement stopped her dead in her tracks. She stared at Harad, her blue eyes blazing. "That's the most disgusting thing I've ever heard."

"Abdul does have his honor," Harad said, teasing her. Now that she was no longer frightened, he found it enjoyable to torment her a little. Her fuse was easy to light. "He wants to be sure I'm satisfied. After all, I did agree to pay a very handsome price for you."

Amelia started to say something then stopped. "How much?" she asked, trying to sound casual.

Harad laughed out loud. Amelia's vanity delighted him. "Far too much," he said. "We'll stay here for the night and set out tomorrow for Alexandria. There are some things I'd like to find out before we leave, though."

"Like who put Abdul up to capturing me?" she asked.

"That's the number one issue," Harad said. "How did you know that?"

"The men who took me mentioned it. What about Tep and Luth? Are they okay?"

"They were beaten, but the injuries weren't life-threatening. Leaving them in the desert could have been fatal, but as it turned out, they'll be fine." Harad picked up the glass Amelia had thrown. He found another and a goatskin filled with wine. He poured two glasses and handed her one. "What did the men say?"

Amelia recounted the snippet of conversation that she'd heard. "It wasn't so much *what* they said as how they said it. It was clear they'd been sent to look for me. Whether it was me as a person or me as a blond female, I can't say."

"As attractive as you are, Amelia, I don't think it was your looks they were after." He couldn't help but smile as he said it.

"Are you implying I'm not attractive enough—"

"To inspire men to kidnap you?" Harad finished the sentence for her. "That isn't the point. How did they know a blue-eyed blonde would be at that place in a vast desert at that particular time?"

"That's exactly what I'd like to know. Only you and Tep and Luth knew when I was going. I didn't tell another soul." She looked at him with suspicion.

"I see," she said.

"Don't be foolish. If I wanted to abduct you, I could have had Tep and Luth do so."

"Someone was watching you, tracking your movements. Now I have to ask you, why that would be?"

Amelia sipped her wine. When she looked up, her blue eyes held mock innocence. "Since I was laboring under the misconception that it was my body they wanted, I don't have a clue what they're really after."

Chapter Nine

Amelia savored the full-bodied wine and the sweet taste of scoring a point on Harad. He'd come to save her, at great trouble to himself, that was true. But he'd sat around that fire with those loathsome men who had looked at her and bargained out a price per pound. Perhaps it was the only option he'd had, but Harad should have given her a sign to let her know what he was up to.

He turned away from her for a moment, and she thought she caught the hint of a smile on his lips. But when he looked at her again, his face held serious concern.

"Amelia, as you know, your sister was almost killed only a few days ago. She is safe now, with my brother," he hastily reminded. "But her research provoked dreams of great wealth and control of world power in several men. With one exception, these men have been captured. If the attacks on you are truly unprovoked because of your own personal interests, they may stem from this last man."

Amelia considered Harad's words. Despite her desire for a little revenge on Harad, she put aside those emotions and thought about what he said. She'd never really considered the how or why of her abduction. Now everything Harad said made sense. Dread crept along her spine.

"I'm not an expert on Beth's work," she admitted. "It always seemed a little stuffy. You know, spending months at an isolated excavation site with no bathrooms, digging in the dirt for chips of pottery and bone."

"I can see that wouldn't appeal to your sense of business," Harad said dryly. "Nonetheless, several people found your sister's research fascinating. Had she been able to find the plant that was used to help my ancestors foretell the future, Beth would have been either very wealthy or very dead."

"But the plant is extinct," Amelia pointed out. "Your mother decided that the risk of continuing to grow it was too dangerous. She destroyed the plant for the safety of the world."

"True." Harad sipped his wine. "But not everyone believes that."

"But why would they think I knew something?" Amelia asked. "Even if I did know it, I probably wouldn't realize I knew it."

Her words caused Harad to frown. "Exactly!" he said, reaching over and grasping her hand. "That's it, Amelia. You know it, and yet you don't know you know it."

"That's good news?" Amelia asked. Harad's finger brushed over the back of her hand, and for a split second she thought only of what it might be like for his feather-soft touch to graze her face. The rush of desire was so strong that she withdrew her hand from his and began to pace the small enclosure of the tent.

"What contact have you had with Beth since she arrived in Egypt?"

"No one in the family even knew Beth was planning an expedition here. She wanted to keep it a secret until she was actually here and the search was moving forward." Amelia shook her head. "Beth has this misconception that I have all the adventures and she's the steady, unexciting member of the family. That just isn't true. I think Beth wanted to surprise everyone in the family by announcing her big find. She called and left a message for me on my answering machine, but I never even spoke to her. Then she sent some photographs, and then later this necklace." She held up the scarab pendant.

"Your sister is a magnet for adventure," Harad agreed. "But you aren't doing so badly yourself." One corner of his mouth quirked up into a grin. "I dare say that if the Egyptian government were fully aware of the trouble you two have caused, you would be banned from my country altogether."

Amelia knew he was baiting her, yet she couldn't resist replying. Her hands went to her hips. "I only came here to see my sister. I'm the one who was abducted, forced to ride halfway across a scorching desert and then sold."

His fingers reached out and caught first one hand and then the other. Holding her lightly, he nodded.

"How true. It's good of you to remind me. You belong to me."

Amelia felt indignation rise. She started to pull her hands free, but when her gaze met Harad's, she halted. There was mischief in his eyes, a dark light that sparkled with pleasure at his ability to rile her. Yet there was something more. She saw his lips part slightly as he, too, felt the impact of their gaze.

"I belong only to myself," she said, the words ragged.

"One day you'll belong to a man. You'll give him your heart and soul, but you will give it willingly."

Her breath was short and shallow, and a flush of heat crept over her skin. He held her hands with the softest pressure, yet she had no desire to pull away from him. Without thought, she took a tiny step toward him.

"Mauve said your family could see the future. Can you?"

"What future would you like to see?" he asked.

"All women dream of happily-ever-after." She took another step toward him. She found it difficult to swallow. Harad's eyes were hypnotic. He was still sitting on the pillows, his gaze locked on hers. Amelia could not look away from his eyes. She had thought him haughty and arrogant at one time. She saw nothing like that as she gazed down at him. What she saw was a hunger that matched her own.

Very slowly he drew her closer to him. He watched her, making sure that she willingly complied with the gentle pressure he put on her hands, stepping so that his face was only inches from her stomach.

Still not breaking the gaze, he released her hands and settled his palms on her waist. Again, the pressure he applied was slight. Amelia found herself yielding to his touch, her body easing down so that she settled in front of him on her knees, their gazes level.

"I can't promise you happily-ever-after. I can only promise you tonight. I can only tell you that I want to kiss you more than I've ever wanted to kiss anyone," he said.

His words were like fire sweeping through her. Amelia melted toward him, barely touching her lips to his. She closed her eyes and opened her mouth, inviting him to kiss her more deeply. She felt his hands move up and around her, his fingertips spreading over her back and ribs.

Outside the tent, musicians had begun to play again. The music was wild and exotic, a throb that Amelia felt in her blood and throughout her entire body. Bracing her with his hands, Harad began to kiss her hungrily.

Her hands grasped his shoulders, holding on to him. He was the only reality in the wild place her desire for him was taking her. One of her hands slipped up his neck and she laced her fingers in his thick hair, pulling him deeper into the kiss.

When he lifted her into his lap, Amelia clung to him. If once she'd thought the fine tailoring of his business suit had implied broad shoulders, she found it to be true. Though he now led the soft life of a businessman, his body was rock hard. He swept her against him, his mouth relinquishing hers only to find the sensitive places of her neck. His lips moved slowly down to her chest. Unable to stop herself, Amelia let her head fall back, giving him full access to her neck and breasts. His lips were hot and urgent, and Amelia heard herself moan.

Shifting her onto the pillow beside him, Harad pulled back, allowing her to open her eyes and look at him.

Amelia tried to slow her breathing, to pull herself together and think. But the dark passion in Harad's eyes pushed all reason and logic away.

When his hand moved to the laces of her top, she touched his cheek.

"Shall we stop?" he asked her.

"No," she answered. "Don't stop."

He pulled the lace, freeing her breasts. The cool air of the desert night teased her superheated skin. The reaction was an invitation Harad did not resist. He bent down, tormenting her with his mouth.

Deftly he untied the skirt, allowing the folds of filmy material to fall away. His hand moved over her belly, making her wild with anticipation.

When he pulled back from her, Amelia reached for him.

"Look at me, Amelia," he said softly.

She opened her eyes.

"You must ask me," he said in a whisper.

"I have to ask?" She searched his face for a hint of teasing.

"Tell me what you want," he answered. His dark gaze burned into her.

Amelia hesitated. The purpose of Harad's request was to force her to confront her own desires. To confront them and verbalize them. To accept her passion as her own. It was a very liberated approach to making love, and very sexy.

"Make love to me, Harad," she said, surprised at the hunger in her voice.

His hand moved lower on her belly. "It will be my pleasure," he said, bending to kiss her with such passion that Amelia forgot everything except his touch.

HE HELD HER in his arms, marveling at the perfection of her body in repose. She slept like a child, deeply and with the hint of a smile. Her blond hair was spread across the pillows and his chest. Very carefully he eased out from beneath her arm and leg and shifted to a sitting position. From that vantage point he could truly appreciate her beauty.

He'd thought of her at first as an ice queen, a woman so controlled, and so controlling, that no passion existed in her except the lust for power.

How wrong he'd been. She'd been hungry and needy and unafraid to show those things to him. Once she gave herself to sensuality, she was more seductive and exciting than any woman he'd ever known. She was a portrait in contrasts.

Gently he brushed a strand of hair from her cheek. She reached up and caught his hand, bringing it to her lips for a kiss.

"Harad," she whispered, reaching for him.

"Yes," he answered, gliding his hand down the silky skin of her arm.

"Is it time to get up?" she asked.

"No." He kissed her forehead. "Sleep a while longer."

"And you?"

"I have something to do."

She opened her eyes, blinking the sleep out of them. "What?" Fully awake, she grasped his hand. "What are you going to do?"

He saw that she was frightened, and he felt a dart of pleasure that she was worried about him. "I shall fulfill my role as the man who bought you." He couldn't help smiling at her look of disapproval.

"And just what will that entail?" she asked, pulling the cotton sheet over her breasts.

"Only the truth," he whispered, leaning down to let his lips graze along her collarbone. She reached out, her fingers catching in his hair and pulling his face up to hers for a kiss. In only a second, the fire between them was rekindled.

Reluctantly, Harad pulled back from her. He teased her full lips with one finger. "I'll return very soon," he promised. "But first I have to explain to Abdul that I have brought the tigress to leash."

At her instant look of outrage, he laughed out loud, moving away from her just in time to avoid being struck by a pillow.

"Whatever you do, don't you dare tell those men

any such thing,'' Amelia said, rising on her elbows. Her blue eyes blazed.

''I've heard it said that a woman is lovely when angered. I never believed it until now.''

''I'm not kidding around, Harad. The last thing you need to do is give those Neanderthals a reason to believe you've made some kind of conquest of a woman you bought.''

''Better for them to believe I conquered you than that I failed. Then they would have no respect for me. They'd never talk with me.'' His mouth twisted up at one corner. ''They'd never drink with me, and I'd never find out how they knew to be waiting for you.'' He grinned at the clear conflict on her face. ''Is your honor worth the knowledge we seek?''

''Perhaps I should get dressed and go find the men and tell them that *I've* conquered *you*.''

Harad laughed out loud. Amelia was not a push-over. ''I would enjoy that very much, but it would not get us the information we need. No matter what you do, Amelia, those men will never accept you as one of them.''

''I know,'' she said, sighing. ''It isn't just here. That's a common attitude all over the world. Some places are just worse than others.''

''But it hasn't hindered you in your climb to the top.''

''I wouldn't say that.'' She shook her hair behind her back. ''I'd say that I've made it as far as I have despite the glass ceiling. That's a term we have in

America for the limit that's put on women. You can see through it, you just can't pass."

Harad had never spent a lot of time thinking about the equality of opportunity. His childhood had been in a tribe where women ruled by birthright. He'd never considered the obstacles Amelia must have faced—and how they'd molded her into the woman she was. "This is a subject I'd like to discuss at a later date. Now, though, I'm going to play the role of desert merchant."

"Desert pig," Amelia corrected.

"If you insist," he said, laughing softly. He went to her and pulled her into his arms for a long kiss. "Wait for me here, just like this. Don't put on a stitch."

"I don't normally take orders, but that's one I think I might enjoy obeying."

"You'll discover, Amelia, that there are many things you'll enjoy."

He turned and exited the tent before he lost all momentum. Looking at Amelia, with her full lips in a pout and her breasts clearly defined by the soft sheets, he knew if he stayed a moment longer he would be back in her embrace.

He took a deep breath as he prepared himself for the boisterous company of the men. One thing was certain, he would never have to pretend that Amelia pleased him. He'd never met a woman who'd made him feel so alive, and so glad to be with her.

THE TENT FLAP OPENS. Exit Harad, desert lover boy. There is a definite swagger to his walk. I'm glad Amelia isn't witnessing this.

All I can say is "At last!" Finally, one of the two lovers has decided to figure out what's going on here. I was beginning to wonder if they were just going to give up on solving the events of the past few days and live on love alone.

I'm telling you, those two are a danger to themselves. If they aren't trying to kill each other in anger, they're about to do a number on themselves in the act of love. They generated enough heat in that tent to light up half of Manhattan. Whew!

I've done a little investigating on my own, and I've come up with some interesting information. Abdul sent a messenger to Alexandria shortly after Harad struck a bargain with him for Amelia.

I think this is a sign we should absolutely get out of Dodge before the bad guys make it here in full force. My theory is that whoever put Abdul up to abducting Amelia isn't going to look kindly on the fact that some stranger has stepped into the picture. Once the discovery is made that the stranger is Harad Dukhan, things are only going to get worse. We need to make an escape. With that in mind, I've gone through Harad's things in the tent where he was supposed to stay and removed the jewel pouch he carried. Good thing, too, because shortly after I did that, one of Abdul's lieutenants slipped into the tent. According to desert hospitality, a thief can't steal from his guest, but I don't buy that. Due to my precautions, the snoop found nothing of value.

I suspect he was looking for gold and jewels, but

he also went through Harad's papers, as if he hoped to find something there other than maps. I'm not reading too much into this. After all, this is a tribe of thieves and caravan muggers. Still, I was troubled by the way the man went through Harad's papers. It was as if he had an idea of what he might find.

Harad has rejoined the men and there is great laughter and backslapping. Ugh! This is the behavior that gets men compared to pigs. Which, I should point out, is greatly unfair to the pig. I haven't had a lot of occasion to make friends with my porcine fellows, but the few pigs I've run into have been very smart and quite witty. I simply can't say that for the majority of humanoids I've known. There are some real nutcases running around out there on two legs.

Even standing twenty feet away from Harad and the boys, I can almost feel the testosterone in the air. And Harad is playing his part to a T. Good thing Amelia can't hear this. She'd blow a gasket for sure.

Abdul is slapping Harad's back, and Harad is reaching into his pocket for some...sapphires. Even at this distance I can see the blue fire in the stones. He's paying a mighty hefty price for Amelia. She should be flattered, but somehow I don't think she'd see it that way.

Good, though. Harad has paid for her, which should relieve Abdul of putting a guard on Amelia and Harad. Up until now, he's been worried that they might try to leave without paying.

Harad is sitting down by the fire. They're passing

a bottle of something. Tea, wine, who knows. Harad is fitting right in. I have to give him credit. Once he shed his business suit, he reverted to his desert heritage. He's quite an actor, and very good at being one of the boys.

Now the conversation has turned serious. Harad is asking the men about various ways to make money. He's hinting that he might want to get into the kidnapping business. He's cleverly bringing the conversation around to who makes good ransom targets and who doesn't. And Abdul is becoming very effusive.

Harad is taking care of business. Now I should go and guard Amelia. Something tells me that she is going to need a lot of help. She has a knack for finding trouble, even when she isn't looking.

Chapter Ten

Harad sipped the strong, hot tea that the men were drinking and listened to the flow of talk. It had become clear to him that Abdul had gone to great pains to arrange the abduction of Amelia based on a very specific request—to detain her for several days until ''someone'' comes to claim her. But no matter how subtly Harad questioned Abdul, he could not get the name of that ''someone''.

Now the chieftain had begun to have second thoughts about his deal with Harad. The American woman's fate seemed to weigh heavily on the desert chief's conscience. To soothe that conscience, Harad spilled the beautiful sapphires into his palm. Once they caught the light of the fire, Abdul's greed far outreached his concern for Amelia. The deal was struck.

With the promise of such a windfall, the men became friendlier. They talked of successful raids and contraband admitting that they sometimes ransomed tourists, but had never ''sold'' anyone before. They were pleased with the profits, which were far superior to common ransoms.

When there was a lull in the conversation, he saw an opportunity to press his point. "I've heard that some raiders specialize in kidnapping travelers for ransom," he said. "I have an interest in making money."

Abdul laughed. "Find an easier way. The risk is too great. This woman is the last for us. Such activity will bring too much scrutiny."

"But it is lucrative," Harad pressed. "I heard that there are scouts in the airport who assess the travelers. They find out about their families. Then they target them for abduction. No one is hurt. The kidnapped person is returned once the money is paid."

Abdul's smile changed to a frown. "You may have heard of such things, but I'm telling you. It isn't a good idea."

"The American woman. She said her family would pay a lot of money for her."

"That's what she said," Abdul admitted. "But she wasn't taken for ransom. Had that been the case, your sapphires would not have tempted me. I only want her gone. I fear she is serious trouble."

Harad knew he'd entered tricky territory. He had to maneuver carefully or Abdul would suspect him. "How did you decide to take her?" he asked. "I thought someone in Alexandria might have alerted you. All I'm asking is for a contact. Who contracted you to share the woman?" He saw the chieftain's face harden and he added, ''I would pay handsomely for a contact.''

''You already have the woman. Isn't that enough?''

Harad laughed out loud. ''She is an expensive acquisition, Abdul. It will take a lot of work to keep her happy.''

''Yes, I can see that. But you don't seem to suffer from a lack of funds.''

Harad shrugged expansively. ''Not today. Tomorrow, though, is unknown. The woman is...persuasive. I have convinced her that her best interests will be served with me. She enjoys the idea of a life of pampering and luxury. I suspect she will be a very costly addition to my household.''

''You can always sell her back to her family,'' Abdul said.

''With her temper, I wonder if they would actually pay to get her back.''

Harad's statement was met with laughter. He continued, ''I believe she will stay with me. By choice. That would make things simpler for me. *And for you.*''

Abdul caught the meaning and nodded. ''You are a smart man.''

''A contact would be greatly appreciated.'' Harad smiled to take any threat out of his request. He knew better than to appear to threaten Abdul, but he also knew to press the only advantage he had, other than money.

''There is a man in Alexandria,'' Abdul said.

"When he contacts me I will ask him if he has an interest in speaking with you."

Harad nodded solemnly. "I will await his answer. I wish to remain in your settlement for another few days, if that's agreeable to you. I would request that your women lavish attention on the American. She has been caught in the spell of adventure, and I want her firmly snagged. I'm hoping in a few days' time she'll forget she had another life. Perhaps by then you can tell me if your associate responds favorably to the idea of working with me."

Abdul's smile was wide. "That would be perfect. I had hoped you would not be in a hurry to leave."

There was the counterthreat, so carefully worded that Harad knew it *could* be accepted as simple hospitality. He knew differently, though. Abdul was telling him not to be in a rush to leave.

Harad rose to his feet. "My thanks for your generous hospitality, Abdul. Now I shall return to my woman."

"Watch your back," Abdul cautioned him. "She has sharp claws and she is very smart."

"You have judged her well," Harad said, bowing before he left.

Walking back to the tent, he knew that he and Amelia had to make a hasty exit. Someone in Alexandria had known of Amelia's plans and had deliberately set Abdul on her. Just as he'd suspected. But waiting around the settlement wouldn't earn him the name of that person. Abdul was no fool. He would give nothing away. Though Harad had been as careful as he knew how, he'd aroused Abdul's suspicions. Someone would be checking on Harad's identity as a merchant. A diligent search would reveal the truth. It was time to leave.

AMELIA ALMOST cried out when the tent flap quivered and a slender form slipped inside.

"Shush!" Ko said, stepping into the circle of light thrown by a lamp. "Are you okay?"

Amelia nodded. She reached for her robe and pulled it over her head, letting the material fall around her body. When she looked at Ko again, she saw that the woman had taken in her situation and was smiling.

"I have been worried for no purpose," Ko said, easing down to a pillow beside Amelia. "You found the merchant to be desirable?"

Amelia felt the blood rush to her cheeks. She must look like a fool, languishing in bed after being bought. "He's okay," she said.

"Sometimes the arrow of love strikes when we least expect it. At least, that's what happened to me."

The words were meant to put Amelia at ease, and they worked. "It's a long story," Amelia said. "One day maybe I can tell you about it."

"One day," Ko agreed. "For now, you should leave here as quickly as you can. Abdul has sent a man to Alexandria. He's going to meet with a man named Nazar Bettina. This is the man who arranged to have you abducted."

"Nazar Bettina!" Amelia felt as if ice water had been drizzled down her spine.

"You know this man?"

"I know of him." Amelia searched the tent until she found her jeans on the floor and began dressing. "He's the man who supposedly paid for my sister's expedition into the desert to find a lost city."

"Abdul is afraid that this man will be angry when he learns that you were sold. This worries me. Abdul was supposed to keep you here, but your merchant paid an enormous price for you. Abdul may decide to call off the bargain, and that would mean trouble for you and your merchant." She lifted her eyebrows. "If you are truly fond of this man, then you should both leave immediately."

There was wisdom in Ko's words, and a lot of courage in her delivery of them. Amelia tied her boot-laces and sat up. "I appreciate your helping me," she said. "I know you're taking a great risk."

Ko bit her bottom lip. "Everyone deserves a chance to plan their own fate."

"I understand." Amelia touched her hand.

"Do you?" Ko asked.

Amelia hesitated. "Maybe not. Is there something you want me to do?"

"Promise me that if I help you and the merchant escape you won't tell the authorities about Abdul and what happened. Because I've seen more of the world than Abdul or the men, I recognize that you're a powerful woman. When you say your family has connections, I know it must be true. If you report the abduction and all that followed, my people will be hunted across the desert. Promise me that if I help you, you'll forget about us."

Amelia weighed what Ko was asking. "What happened was wrong. If Ha—the merchant hadn't come along, there's no telling what would have happened to me."

"Abdul wouldn't have harmed you. He would have held you until Nazar Bettina arrived."

"And then?" Amelia felt goose bumps slide up her arms at the possibility.

"I can't answer that. But I can promise you that Abdul would not have involved his people if he'd thought violence would come to you. I can't say what this Nazar Bettina told him. I can only promise that no one else will be abducted. My husband has talked with the other men of the tribe. The majority of the men are opposed to continued kidnapping. Abdul will listen to them in the future."

"How can I find this Nazar Bettina?" Amelia recalled that he was the only person who hadn't been rounded up when the authorities rescued Beth and Omar. Though an intensive search had been launched by the Egyptian authorities, it was discovered that Nazar Bettina was an alias. The man behind the name had never been found.

"He lives in Alexandria. He's a wealthy man. That's all I know."

"Have you ever seen him?" Amelia pressed.

"Perhaps," Ko said. "There was a man who visited here once. I think that was him, but no one ever told me. He was tall and handsome. Dark eyes and hair.'' She made a wry face. ''Like ninety percent of all of the men around here.''

''Would you recognize him if you saw him again?''

''I don't know. I saw him walking past, and I'm not even certain it was him.''

''I need to find him,'' Amelia said.

''I can't help you with that. But I will have your horses saddled and provisions packed. It's all that I can do.''

Amelia nodded. ''It's a lot, Ko. You've been a friend to me. You have my word that I won't pursue Abdul. I can't vouch for what Bettina may do or say once he's cornered. But it won't come from me.''

Ko's smile was relieved. ''The horses will be ready an hour before dawn. I'll come for you and take you to them.''

''Could you do one other favor?'' Amelia asked. ''Attach the wicker carrying case to the back of my saddle. I don't want to leave the black cat.''

''Yes,'' Ko said. ''He's your luck charm. He watches over you and the merchant. He's a very intelligent animal.''

''Yes, he most certainly is,'' Amelia agreed.

IT'S NICE TO KNOW the fan club is growing, but the idea of spending another eight or ten hours on horseback is more than I can bear. Ugh. I guess the only option is to remain here, and I think I'd just as soon depart.

Nazar Bettina. The mystery man from Beth's past. Mr. Deep Pockets. I had a bad feeling when they rounded up all the other bad guys and he escaped that we'd hear from him again.

The Alexandria police did an intensive search for this man and there was no record of his existence. No one could discover the real name of Beth's generous backer, or what his motives might have been. But that question must be answered, because it bears on why Bettina would be interested in Amelia. Either he doesn't believe that the plant that assisted in telling the future is extinct, or he thinks there's something else to be gained by following up on Beth's research.

Beth is safely in the desert with Omar. I have to believe that she's beyond Bettina's clutches or he would be after her instead of Amelia.

What could Amelia know about Beth's work that would interest Bettina? She claims to know nothing. If there is something, then we can figure out the best path to take to find this Bettina person and put him behind bars.

I suppose I'll have to check through Amelia's things myself. If you want a job done, then you have to do it correctly. That's the motto that's made me a successful feline detective.

Amelia is throwing her things together. So far, nothing looks interesting, but I'll have to give them a thorough going-over before I can draw that conclusion. And there's no time like the present to get busy.

AMELIA GATHERED up her things, including the dancing costume. She held it in her hands, hesitating about packing it.

"I earned it," she said out loud and tossed it into the backpack. She looked up when the black cat snagged it with a paw and pulled it out.

"Hey!" she said.

The cat ignored her. Discarding the diaphanous dancing costume, he pulled out her clothes and shoes and rooted deeper into the bag.

"Hey! Cut it out!" she ordered.

Familiar disappeared in the backpack. When he came out, he went to the side pockets and began using his teeth to open them.

"What's going on?" Harad asked as he entered the tent and saw a pair of socks flying out of the backpack.

"It's Familiar. I was packing, but he decided to unpack," Amelia said.

"He's hunting for something," Harad said. "Probably the same thing I'm wondering about. Abdul admitted that you were a deliberate target. He wouldn't say the name of the person who set up the abduction."

"Nazar Bettina," Amelia supplied. "I thought he didn't exist."

"Not under that name." Harad's tone was worried. "How did you find out?"

"Ko," Amelia said. "She's willing to help us leave here if I won't sic the authorities on Abdul for kidnapping me."

"And?"

"I agreed," Amelia said.

"Good thinking. We have to be far away from here before this man, whoever he is, arrives. I don't know what he wants with you, but he's gone to a tremendous amount of trouble to have you captured and held here."

"It has to do with Beth's research, but I don't know a thing about it."

Harad nodded. "I feel certain that's what's behind all this. Beth never spoke to you about her work or this trip?"

"No, never." Amelia turned back to the cat as a pair of panties landed on the rug at her feet. "She did send me something, though."

Familiar's head popped out of the backpack. "Meow?"

Amelia went to the small leather purse she carried and pulled out the padded packet. "She sent these." She opened the packet and spilled the prints out onto the pillows.

The black-and-white prints showed a series of strange hieroglyphics. The pages were numbered in order, and Amelia laid them out. "I've looked at them several times and I don't have a clue what they are. There was no explanation when they arrived. But they must mean a lot to Beth."

"They're very valuable to some people," Harad said softly.

"Do you know what they mean?" Amelia asked as she gathered them back up and returned them to her purse.

"Beth used a sophisticated underwater camera to record those images in a sunken city off the cost of Alexandria. She believed that if she could decipher the hieroglyphics, she would have the directions to the lost City of Con."

"So, they're like some kind of treasure map," Amelia said.

"Exactly."

"And is there gold and silver and jewels in this lost city?"

"Yes, but I don't believe that's the treasure Bettina is after."

"He's still after the plant! The orbus! But it's extinct," Amelia pointed out.

"Bettina obviously doesn't believe that to be true. If that plant were still being cultivated, it could be worth billions of dollars. Imagine what a pharmaceutical company could do with a drug like that. A man like Bettina must find it difficult to believe that my people would destroy what ultimately would be a fortune."

Amelia picked up the packet. "You think Nazar Bettina may be after these?"

"He funded Beth's trip to find the lost City of Con. I believe that finding the orbus was the real goal. If that assumption is true, then Bettina has been trying to retrieve those images. That's why you were attacked in the airport. Your luggage was slashed open, remember?"

"That makes sense, but I thought the plant only worked on people of your bloodline," Amelia said.

"Maybe, maybe not." Harad picked up the packet of images. "Only those of my bloodline were *allowed* to take the drug. It was thought that it would kill any others who attempted it."

"No one else even tried?" Amelia was incredulous.

"This was a long time ago," Harad reminded her. "The belief in birthright and divine rule was very strong. The worship of gods and goddesses was practiced almost without exception. People didn't defy their gods, as they do now. As far as I know, no one outside the lineage of Con ever tried the drug."

"And your mother? Did it work for her?"

Harad hesitated. "I don't know. She would never admit to trying the drug. She said it didn't exist anymore, that the world had grown too small. If the power of prophecy fell into the wrong hands, one man could rule the entire planet."

There was something in Harad's voice that made Amelia examine his face. "You don't think the plant is extinct, do you?" She felt her gut twist at the possibility.

"I never doubted my mother's word."

"But you do now?" she pressed.

"I have to wonder if somewhere in the lost city, there aren't some seeds preserved."

"Harad, if the wrong person got hold of them—"

"We can't let that happen, Amelia. We simply have to stop this Bettina before it's too late."

Chapter Eleven

Before leaving the tent, Amelia stopped for a last look around. Ko had already come and gone. The horses were provisioned and waiting. Though Amelia was packed, she decided to leave her belongings, with the exception of the pictures Beth had sent her. It was time to leave.

Amelia's gaze fell on the cushions that had been her bed. And Harad's. It seemed impossible that only hours before, they'd been in each other's arms. It had been so natural, so right. And once they were back in Alexandria and safe, what would happen between them? Amelia's world was centered in Manhattan. Harad's was Alexandria. In more than geography, they were worlds apart. What could the future hold for two people as different as they were? It was a question Amelia didn't want to answer.

"Amelia," Harad said softly.

"I'm ready," she answered.

He came up behind her, his arms slipping around to hold her. "If Bettina weren't coming, you could stay here. I'd come back for you. Abdul won't hurt you, but you must get back to Alexandria. It's urgent.''

She saw worry in his eyes. ''I want to go with you. I can't stay here.''

''Then why are you looking so sad?'' he asked.

''I just wanted to remember.'' She turned in his arms and looked up at him. ''I never want to forget what we shared here.'' Even the memory of it made her hungry for another kiss.

''If you forget, I know ways to remind you,'' Harad said, kissing her upturned lips.

For a long moment, Amelia held on to him. There was a promise in his words, no matter how vague. He implied there would be a time and place for reminders. Now there was no time for romance, but she knew that the long night ahead of her would require something to hold on to. Harad was it.

She stepped slightly back from him, breaking the embrace. ''I know we have to go.''

''If we get away without being detected, we'll have a good hour's lead.''

''Will they really follow us?''

''Maybe not,'' he said. But she knew by the way Harad turned away that they would be pursued. Hotly pursued. She hadn't realized how much she was worth to Abdul—or rather to Bettina—until that moment.

''We could leave the hieroglyphics,'' she suggested. ''No one will ever be able to interpret them.''

''Your sister and Mauve had come close to figuring out part of the code. No, before we allow the photos to fall into the wrong hands, we'll have to destroy them."

"That might be the best idea," Amelia said.

"I'd prefer to keep them. I need to analyze them myself. Even we if destroy the images, the temple and the carvings are still beneath the sea."

"Would you consider destroying that?" Amelia asked. She'd given up on thinking any accomplishment was beyond Harad's reach. His family had protected the secrets of Con for centuries. They would continue to do so.

"Perhaps it would be simpler to thoroughly check the lost city and make sure that nothing dangerous remains there."

She nodded. That was the best plan. Sooner or later, someone would stumble across the lost City of Con. Beth had already come close to finding it, and there would be others. The earth had become a small planet.

Harad clasped her hand in his. "Shall we?"

She smiled at the way he made it sound like an invitation to dance.

"Lead on," she said. She raised her eyebrows when Harad led her to the back of the tent and cut a slit for them to slip through, with a dagger he seemed to produce from nowhere. Amelia was surprised at the silence that surrounded the settlement. She'd never imagined that the bustling village of tents and children, horses and camels, could become so peaceful under the starlit sky.

Harad's strong hand held hers, and Amelia followed him when he gently pulled her away from the tent they'd shared so briefly and into a jog. Like shadows, they slipped from cover to cover. Familiar darted, seeming to watch for guards.

As Ko had promised, Pooldar and a fine-boned bay mare stood tethered side by side nearly a hundred yards west of the camp. To Amelia's immense relief, the wicker basket was attached to her saddle, and as she approached, Familiar flipped up the lid and settled in to watch them.

"Meow!" he complained.

"Sorry to keep you waiting," Harad whispered, scratching the cat's head as he reached for the mare's reins. With one smooth movement he lifted Amelia into the saddle.

"How good a rider are you?" he asked.

"Good enough," she said.

Harad's smile was his only answer. He swung up on Pooldar's back and without a word pushed the stallion into a gallop.

Amelia pressed her heels into the mare's ribs and leaned forward in the saddle, the wind whistling in her ears as the little mare galloped after Harad with a surge of speed.

Amelia caught up with Harad in no time, and side by side they raced through the sand and toward a horizon of black velvet night spangled with stars.

OH, GREAT, it's the Perrelli twins. They forget that sitting on the rump of the horse is a little different than being able to ride in the saddle. Thank goodness

Ko thought to put a soft rug in this basket, or I'd be nothing but bruises by the time we stop.

I guess I should be thankful the humanoids were smart enough to make an escape. Once they became enamored of each other, I was afraid they might zip the tent flap shut and forget they were in danger.

While I'm being bounced all over the place, I might as well indulge in a bit of philosophizing. I find it interesting that Harad and Amelia finally saw each other in the glow of Cupid's lantern, so to speak.

They're both highly competitive humanoids. Amelia can honestly worry the warts off a frog with her sassy attitude. And Harad, he's the kind of man who snaps his fingers and women jump. They are the antithesis of each other's dream mate. Yet they have a chemistry between them that could blow up the lab. I, of course, being a trained observer, saw it from the outset. But I honestly never thought they'd get it together. It was more likely that they'd have each other thrown in jail.

The ways of love are mysterious indeed. Beth and Omar were a natural. They both had a love of adventure and the preservation of the past to bind them together. They'll make a fine couple, and I have no doubts that Beth will adapt to the life of a desert chieftain's wife while retaining her own career.

Amelia, though, she's a city gal. I wonder if she could ever find a simple life as satisfying as being the big dog in a business meeting. Then again, Harad prefers the challenges of the business world to life in the sand. As wise as I am to human nature, I won't hazard a guess what the future of these two will be.

If Harad presents himself as a challenge, Amelia won't be able to resist. If she sets her heels and acts mulish, Harad won't be able to walk away from her until he's won her over. A relationship built on challenges. Well, I've seen a lot worse.

At last, the horses are slowing. Although I'm not certain I don't prefer the canter to the trot. It's a good thing I didn't eat a lot before this trip. Speaking of eating, I've been sadly neglecting that part of my routine. I think I must have lost at least three pounds. As soon as we get safely to Alexandria, I'm going to demand the finest meal in town.

The Abbula Hotel had some spectacular dishes. I can only hope Eleanor and Peter are still there and waiting for me. I doubt the reception is going to be warm, but once I'm returned to their arms, they'll forgive me—and feed me. I just have to get these two back to the city safe and sound and then we have to find this Bettina character. I never should have assumed that the world was safe until he was behind bars.

At last, we've slowed to a walk. This feels so much better. As long as we keep this gait up, I can take a little kitty nap. This gentle rocking is quite pleasant. I'll curl up and sleep for a while so that I'm refreshed and ready to detect as soon as I wake up.

HARAD REACHED over and slipped Amelia's reins over the horn. She was asleep in the saddle, her head falling forward. It had been a long eight hours of hard riding, but so far there was no sign that anyone was following them. By his calculations, they would make the outskirts of Alexandria in another hour.

He patted Pooldar's neck, making certain the stallion wasn't overheated. The cool night had given way to a broiling sun, and now the horses walked slowly. Harad knew they were as tired as he was. But not as worried. He had to get Amelia to the hospital for further tests.

Dropping back slightly, he lifted the lid of the wicker basket to check on Familiar. The cat's golden-green eyes blinked up at him.

"We're almost there," he informed the cat.

Familiar nodded, his whiskers twitching.

Harad dropped the lid back. At least the wicker basket provided some shade for the cat. There was no relief for him or Amelia. Just the promise of Alexandria, a hot bath, some food and access to his resources. The man who used the name Nazar Bettina would be found. Harad would not rest until he was unmasked.

A quick breeze kicked up, blowing the sand along the crest of a nearby dune. Harad welcomed the breeze. It was a momentary relief from the baking sun. The desert was a place of such extremes. He'd forgotten some of its savage beauty since he'd adopted the life of a businessman. There were memories, though. Good ones.

As a young boy, he'd been caught with his mother in a windstorm. The power of the wind, howling over the dunes, had been terrifying. Only his mother's quick thinking and knowledge of the desert had saved them. They'd found refuge and survived. He could still remember his fear as he'd pressed into his mother. She'd wrapped her arms around him and then a piece of material, shutting out the blowing sand. What had seemed like eternity had been only twenty minutes. Huddled together at the base of a dune, Harad and Aleta and the horses had managed to survive. When it was over, Harad had crept out of the comfort of his mother's arms to view a vista that had been completely changed by the storm.

No, he wasn't likely to forget the power of the wind and the way it could sweep over the desert, seemingly out of nowhere.

He watched the plumes of sand on the crest of the dune. They were a little odd. Pooldar shifted under him, his ears pricking forward and his attention turning to the top of the dune.

Harad stopped the stallion. The little bay instantly stopped beside him. Familiar's head popped out of the basket, and his attention, too, was turned to the dune.

"Amelia," Harad said, reaching a hand onto her thigh to steady her as she awakened.

"What?" She sat up straight, fully alert.

"The dune." Harad nodded toward it. Now all was quiet.

"What is it?"

"There's someone on the other side of it."

"Are you sure?" She sat taller in her saddle for a better look.

"I'm positive. Someone is there."

"What are we going to do?" She gathered her reins and stretched her legs down into the stirrups, making sure her seat was steady in case they needed to run.

"Turn your horse to the east," Harad said. They'd been traveling in a northerly direction. "Just make it slow and easy."

Amelia did exactly as he requested. The bay mare made a gentle correction. Harad kept Pooldar beside her. But the stallion's attention was still on the dune.

"Don't look at the dune. Pretend we're just continuing with our journey as before," Harad said. "I don't know who is back there, but they know we're here."

"How can you be certain?" Amelia asked. "I didn't see anyone."

"Listen to me, Amelia. Keep riding east. Once you're in the city, call my office. Tell them what happened. They'll help you. And call Dr. Mosheen. He needs to speak with you." He saw the fear on her face and knew that it wasn't for her own safety. Amelia was worried about him.

"You sound as if you won't be with me. I'm not going anywhere without you."

"They want *you,* Amelia. They're not interested in me. I'm going to try and divert them long enough for you to get ahead of them."

"No."

He knew by that one word that Amelia had made up her mind and that it was going to take a lot to make her listen to him. "You don't have a say in this. Just once, do as I ask you. I need for you to ride. Just ride.'' The man called Nazar Bettina had gone to a lot of trouble to get Amelia. If he honestly believed she knew something, Harad wasn't certain how far he would go to get that information. Amelia could not be caught. ''If you have any regard for my safety, you'll do as I ask.''

''I'm not leaving you.'' Her chin was in the air and her jaw set. He didn't have to see her blue eyes to know they were blazing.

Harad felt his patience grow thin, but he knew Amelia well enough to know that he couldn't order her to do anything. ''They won't hurt me. They're after you.''

Amelia reached across to touch his hand that held Pooldar's reins. ''I won't leave you, Harad. You're in this because of me. I'm not about to turn tail and run now that the bad guys are closing in on us.''

''You won't be running away from them, you'll be avoiding capture. Pooldar is stronger and faster than your horse. Make a run for it and I'll catch up with you.''

He could almost see the wheels of her brain turning as she considered his words. He was used to people doing as he instructed. Men, women and children. He didn't issue an order unless it was necessary, and sensible people understood that. Amelia was as far from sensible as anyone he'd ever met.

''No,'' she finally said. ''I think you're fibbing to try and keep me safe.''

Harad tightened his hand on the saddle horn.

"Okay, then, we'll ride together," he said, "but if you can't keep up, they're going to get both of us."

"You underestimate me and my horse," Amelia said, the challenge in her eyes. "Let's go." She put her heels to the mare's side and they jumped forward. Harad was right on her heels.

He looked back to see a lone rider top the crest of the dune. The man wore the flowing desert robes and rode a proud gray Arabian stallion. The horse pranced as the man held binoculars to his face and stared at Harad.

Harad had just begun to believe he was alone when two other riders topped the dune. Instead of giving pursuit, they simply watched as Harad and Amelia galloped away from them.

Amelia looked back over her shoulder to make sure Harad was coming. All of the challenge was gone from her face, replaced by worry. It struck Harad that for all of her mulishness, she'd been unwilling to leave him, not because she was stubborn and willful, but because she cared what happened to him. Which was exactly the same reason he'd been so determined to see her safe.

Her face registered surprise when she saw the three riders simply watching them, making no effort to chase them down. Still, she didn't slow her horse. She kept at a gallop with Harad right on her heels.

It wasn't until they'd put some miles between themselves and the men on the dune that they finally slowed and let the horses catch their breath.

"What was that all about?" Amelia asked.

"I don't know," Harad admitted. "If their horses were fresh, they could have caught us."

"They didn't even try. Maybe they weren't interested in us at all."

"Maybe," Harad said, though he didn't believe it. The men had been watching them intently.

"Well, we've got a good head start on them. How far to Alexandria?"

Harad corrected their position and calculated the distance. "Another half hour." Both Pooldar and the mare were winded and blowing. They needed water and shade. They were tough horses, but they'd been ridden hard for the past several days.

"Do you think it's safe for us to rest?" Amelia asked, patting her mare's neck. "Even if we just got off and walked for a short distance it might help them."

Harad weighed the horses' condition against the feeling in his gut that something bad was about to happen. "We'd best keep riding," he said. "We'll take it slow." He didn't add that he wanted to be mounted and ready, should anything go wrong. To his relief, Amelia didn't argue.

The wicker lid inched up, and Familiar looked out. The cat turned in the direction of Alexandria, and Harad felt a tiny measure of relief. Familiar didn't act as if anything was wrong. Cats were supposed to be psychic, or at least extremely sensitive to danger.

"Did Dr. Mosheen say what kind of tests he wanted to run?" Amelia asked.

"He didn't specify." Harad kept his tone casual.

"You think those riders didn't chase us because they didn't have to. We're headed exactly where they knew we'd go."

Harad had underestimated Amelia's awareness of the situation.

"It's possible," he admitted.

"We could circle the outskirts of the city and approach from a different direction, but the horses won't make it," Amelia said.

Harad was impressed with her thinking. She faced the situation squarely, without flinching. "Even if the horses were fresh, I don't think it would do any good. I suspect wherever we enter the city, someone will be waiting for us."

"For me," Amelia said quietly. "You act like you're part of this, Harad, but you're not. You'd be safe in your office if you hadn't gotten involved with me. You may pretend that isn't true, but I know it is."

"I gave my brother and your sister my word that I would protect you and see you safely back on the plane to Paris. I'm honor-bound to do that."

"Your honor doesn't require that you die for me." Amelia reined her mount to a standstill. When Harad was beside her she put her hand on his thigh, urging him with her touch to stop. "I don't expect you to spend the rest of your life protecting me."

She was so sincere and brave that Harad almost couldn't resist.

"What if that's the way I choose to spend my time?" he asked.

Amelia looked directly into his eyes. "I'd say you were a man who enjoyed thankless tasks," she answered.

Harad's laughter was long and loud, and it relieved the tension that had built up in him. "A glutton for punishment is the phrase I've heard," he said, still laughing.

Harad leaned over until his lips brushed her cheek. "Call me a fool, but nothing will prevent me from protecting you, not even your own hardheadedness."

Chapter Twelve

When Alexandria finally appeared on the horizon, Amelia felt like Dorothy when she first glimpsed Oz. No place had ever looked so good—or so unattainable. Miles of desert seemed to stretch before her.

"If I had ruby slippers I could click my heels together and go home," she said, then gave Harad a rueful smile. "Sorry, an old American movie."

"*The Wizard of Oz,* Judy Garland." Harad identified the reference.

"You know that movie?" she asked.

"Though I grew up in the desert, my education and cultural exposure were not neglected," Harad said. "My mother made certain that both Omar and I would be able to function in the world outside our desert home. We made frequent trips to cities in Europe, and as I told you earlier, we were both formally educated in Paris."

"Why did you leave the desert?" Amelia asked. It was a question that had been niggling at her. Though he was the consummate businessman, he was also the wild desert warrior. She'd seen him galloping across the dunes on Pooldar. Even though he'd left his childhood behind, he would never completely rid himself of his desert heritage. Nor, she thought, did he really want to.

"I would think you'd understand perfectly. With my people, the role of leader was handed to me. I was born to it. I never did a thing to earn it. In the world of business, a man—or woman—excels by his or her own merits. I liked the challenge of business, and then I fell in love with design, the study of architecture. Form and function. To create something new and suited exactly for the purpose it serves, yet is also beautiful—I became addicted to the thrill of it. Dukhan Enterprises allows me to design a building and then create it. It is very satisfying."

"I know," Amelia agreed. "For me, the business world became a place where I could prove myself. I could come up with creative ideas and bring in the big clients just like the guys. Although, when I first started out, this one company used to send me out to work with clients. I quickly caught on that the men weren't interested in my ideas for advertising campaigns. They had something else entirely on their minds. I guess I've been trying to prove that I'm not just a bauble ever since." Amelia had never intended to admit such a thing, but as they continued riding through the afternoon sun, exhausted, she found it easy to talk to Harad.

"Do you regret how you spent your time?"

"No," she answered, weighing her words. "But I

didn't have to give up anything. You gave up a lot—a way of life, a position of leadership. A lot."

"Each person has to make choices in life. We all have to select our priorities. I saw my mother choose her role as leader over her role as wife to my father. I guess for a long time I couldn't forgive her that."

"Because she was a woman?"

"Because she was my mother. And because it drove my father away from us."

It was an honest answer. Perhaps too honest. "If your father had made the same choice, would you have felt the same?" Amelia knew she was playing devil's advocate, but the answer was very important to her. The different expectations placed on women were pervasive in society. A woman with high ambitions was considered unnatural, while a man with the same ambitions was applauded as a go-getter.

Harad didn't answer immediately. Instead, he glanced at Amelia and studied her face. "Is this a test?"

"Yes," she said, "but there is no correct answer. There's only the truth."

"For you, there's only one answer," Harad said.

Amelia didn't deny it. Harad was right, and there was no point in pretending otherwise. She couldn't change who she was, not even for him.

"For a long time I blamed my mother. That isn't true any longer. I see that I was unfair to her. I wanted what I saw other boys had, a mother who put her husband and children first. That wouldn't have satisfied my mother. Why should she have been forced to give up her dream?''

Amelia heard her heart thumping in her ears. She'd been holding her breath, waiting for Harad's answer.

''What I blame both of my parents for is not realizing they weren't suited. My father had expectations that were unreal. I knew my mother well enough to know she never lied to him or led him on. He believed marriage and motherhood would change her. He was wrong. And my mother should have found a man who was willing to accept her choices.''

She heard the slimmest edge of bitterness in his voice and knew that he had suffered greatly over the breakup of his family.

''Then she wouldn't have had you and Omar. You're who you are because of your parents. Let me ask you another question. Do you think either of your parents regretted the choices they made?''

Again Harad took his time answering. Before he did, he stopped Pooldar and reached across to capture her hand. He brought it swiftly to his lips and kissed her palm. ''No, Amelia, I don't think they regretted a single moment. And I thank you for reminding me of that. My parents loved each other. Perhaps that's the only thing that matters.''

The sun had begun to slip behind the horizon, and the sky was filled with a pink light that seemed to make Harad's dark eyes luminous as he gazed at her.

''I think loving someone is the only thing that matters.'' She gave a half chuckle and shook her head in a self-deprecating manner. ''Two days ago I would never have said that. I wouldn't even have allowed myself to believe it. But you've made me see the truth of it."

Harad nudged Pooldar into a walk and the mare stayed by his side. "We both have much to teach each other."

"But will we have time for those lessons?" she asked, realizing that her voice trembled.

Harad's fingers closed on her hand before he released it. "There is no power that can stop us, if that's what we choose."

It was an artful dodge. Harad was a man who'd lived without commitment to anyone or anything except his own success. Amelia knew that for the first time in her life she was looking into a mirror that gave back her own reflection. Only this wasn't the image she wanted to see.

She was caught up in images of the past—Harad's bare chest lit by candles in the darkness of the tent, his eyes staring into hers with a hunger that made her feel as if her skin would catch fire, the little smile that softened his features when he touched her and the way he wove his fingers into her hair and held on to her.

It seemed that she'd never felt such desire for a man, or such need. Harad was a craving. She wanted to ride up beside him and feel his touch again. The brush of his hand over hers was enough to sustain her. His kiss was a feast.

As the fevered images slipped through her mind, she realized that she'd lost control of her emotions.

Without any warning, she'd fallen in love with a man she barely knew. She'd watched other women suddenly give up career dreams and goals to marry and have families. The process had always amazed her. Not that marriage and motherhood weren't good things, but she'd never understood how a woman so focused on career could suddenly do a one-eighty. Now she understood. He was in her blood.

She could barely remember the details of her important business deal in Paris, but she recalled every shift of expression on Harad's face when he made love to her. The time they'd shared together had become more important than anything else in her life.

The entire experience was terrifying.

She gripped the saddle horn as weariness spread through her body. She was suddenly very tired, but Harad's next words sent a surge of adrenaline through her.

"It is still a distance to safety," Harad said, pointing toward the scattering of outlying buildings that was the outskirts of Alexandria. "We've made it, but we're not alone."

"Where?" Amelia was careful not to show a reaction to his words.

"To the west, just behind that third building."

A strange silence had fallen over the sparsely settled area. The only sound was the lowing of several sheep farther down the road.

She felt the lid of the wicker basket press against her back. Familiar was staring at a deep doorway on the right. A low growl issued from his throat.

Amelia didn't see the man until he darted from the alcove to the next building. His actions were furtive, and she felt goose bumps dance lightly over her skin.

"What shall we do?" she asked.

"Keep moving," Harad said firmly. "We'll find a phone, and I'll have someone from my office meet us with a car."

The horses walked through the quiet streets, their hooves echoing in the eerie silence. Amelia realized it was sundown, a time for prayer. That would explain the quietness of the streets, but it did little to calm her jumpy nerves. She expected a band of thugs to jump out from behind each building they passed, but there were only a few men bustling down the street and a solitary woman carrying goods in a basket.

The deeper into the city they went, the more crowded the buildings became. Though Amelia searched the shadows on either side of the road, she didn't see the man who'd been watching them.

Harad stopped at a house. He left Amelia holding Pooldar's reins while he went to the door and spoke with a woman. He pressed money into her hand and was back at Amelia's side in little more than a minute.

"Some of my staff will be here soon," he said, leading Pooldar and her mare off the road and behind the modest home. "The woman said there was water out here." He spotted a watering trough in the middle of a goat pen and led the horses toward it. They drank eagerly, and Harad carefully monitored the amount.

Amelia slipped to the ground, landing lightly on

her feet. "Why doesn't that man do something?" she asked.

Harad frowned. "He's keeping tabs on us and biding his time. They'll pick the place to attack when they have the advantage. Or when they have you alone."

Amelia used her hands to cup some water and drink, then signaled Harad to open the wicker basket so she could offer Familiar some. The black cat lapped the water with enthusiasm. When he was finished, he jumped to the ground. Stretching mightily, he began to walk around, his gaze constantly going back to the road, his attention focused on a two-story building about a hundred yards away.

"Do you think Familiar really knows someone is watching us?" Amelia asked.

"I have no doubt," Harad answered. He shifted the horses so they formed some protection for Amelia.

"None of this makes sense." Amelia couldn't control the frustration in her voice. She was tired of being stalked, but her feelings for Harad also played into her sense that she'd lost control of her life.

"Why would they go to the trouble of having me abducted in the desert and then not make an attempt to snatch me before we call the police?" she asked.

"In the desert there would be no trace of your disappearance. People disappear in the sand. Accidents happen. Plus, everything would point to Abdul if there were any investigation. Here—" he waved a hand around "—there would be questions from officials. They would also have to abduct me. Whoever is doing this wants something from you, Amelia, and they don't want the entire police force looking for you, or me."

"You'd be missed, I suppose," Amelia agreed.

"By my competitors, if no one else," Harad said with a small degree of humor.

"But you think they'll try something again?"

"I'm positive of it. But we'll be ready for them the next time."

His words were meant to reassure her, but they didn't. "What happens if I just leave?"

Harad shrugged. "Maybe nothing. Then again, if I'm correct in assuming that Nazar Bettina is the man behind all of this, he may go after your sister. He wants something, and he put up a lot of money to try and get it. You're the easier target now. If you leave, he'll have to go after Beth again."

"Can he find her?" Amelia couldn't suppress the worry in her voice. She'd never considered that Beth was still in danger. She'd assumed her sister was safely tucked away in some desert oasis, moments from being wedded to a sheik.

"Five years ago, I would have said no. Today, with the technology available to any buyer, I'm certain he can."

"You'd think he'd be smart enough to keep looking for Beth. I don't know anything." Amelia felt her anger surge. "He must not be as smart as he thinks he is."

"I wouldn't look at it like that," Harad said. "You're here in Egypt, which means you know something. And even if you don't, then once he has you, he has a bargaining chip to get the information he wants. Beth and Omar would trade any secret to keep you safe. This man knows he'll need leverage to get what he wants. I'd say he's a pretty smart man."

The last bit of light was fading from the sky, and Amelia saw a pair of headlights coming down the road.

"That's my car," Harad said. He stepped in front of Amelia, a fact that wasn't lost on her. Harad was taking no chances, not even with his own people.

The car drove slowly toward them, and when it finally pulled level, a man armed with an automatic jumped out of the car. He quickly surveyed the surrounding area as two other men came out of the car with weapons drawn.

Amelia was reluctant to turn her little mare over to the stranger who appeared at her side, but she gave him the reins.

"Take good care of her," Amelia said. "She did a great job." She stooped down to lift the cat into her arms.

Amelia saw Harad nod, and one of the men assisted her into the back seat of the limo. She scooted over to make room for Harad, but one of the armed men slipped onto the seat beside her.

"Take her to the office," Harad said.

"Hey!" Amelia protested. "Aren't you coming?"

"First I'm going to see if I can trap our observant little friend," Harad said. In the darkness she saw the flash of his white teeth. "I'm tired of being the prey. It's time to reverse the roles and become the hunter."

"Let me stay with you." She hated the pleading note in her voice. Never before in her life had she ever begged a man for anything.

"It isn't safe," Harad said. "My men will take you to the office. There's a suite of rooms there. They'll see that you have food and drink, and something for Familiar. He looks famished. After you refresh yourself, if I'm not there, you need to go straight to the hospital." He grimaced. "Dr. Mosheen wants to do the tests on you as soon as possible."

"I'm not hungry and I feel fine. I'm not—"

"Just go let the doctor check you out. Please, Amelia. You look perfectly fine, but why take a risk?"

"You're the one taking risks, and I can't let you take any more for me," she insisted. "I want to be here to help you."

Harad leaned into the window so that he was only inches from her face. "I'll be with you soon," he promised.

"Harad," she said, a warning in her tone, "don't do this. Don't have me carted off like a child."

One of the armed men whispered something briefly in Harad's ear, drawing his attention to the two-story building Familiar had been watching.

"Don't act like a child," he replied.

"I won't—"

"There's no time to argue." He pulled back and tapped the top of the limo twice. It pulled away before she could say anything else. She turned to look out the rear window and saw the dim outline of Harad and one man as they stood beside the horses, their heads together, scheming.

MADAME TAURUS IS in a fine frenzy of fury. Not exactly the alliteration my idol, E. A. Poe, would create, but it'll do in a pinch.

Now that I'm sitting in air-conditioned comfort, reclining on cool leather seats with the promise of a good meal, I'm feeling much better. Even a bit philosophical. Most people don't realize that Poe was the inventor of the mystery. He's commonly remembered for his poetry and stories of horror, but it was The Murder in the Rue Morgue *that many classify as the first real mystery.*

As I recall, there was much made over inductive and deductive reasoning in that story. It's my firm belief that a good P.I. must have both.

Hence, I have deduced that if Amelia could get her hands on Harad, she could tear his throat out. Her emotions are all out of whack, and like all unreasonable bipeds, she's going to blame him for that. She wants him, and for the first time in her life she realizes that something she wants may not be hers for the asking. He isn't a merger or a deal or a new contract. He isn't something she can conquer with intellect. Harad won't be won by logic—and he isn't one that's going to be easy to manipulate. Just the opposite. He's going to do exactly the thing that most drives her nuts.

And it only makes her want him more.

Humans are perverse, you see. Poe understood that well. It's why he's such a great writer.

We're pulling up to the front of Dukhan Enterprises. Yes, Harad does have a suite of rooms here. Quite a lovely suite, as I recall from my first visit just few weeks ago, on Beth's behalf. And an irascible feline named Tut. Now, what was his assistant's name? Jasmine? Lola? No, something simpler. Marie. That's it.

The armed men are letting us out and escorting us inside. I feel like a dignitary. I like that limo. I wonder if Peter and Eleanor would consider getting one for me? Doubtful, but it never hurts to ask. I'll give them a hello as soon as I make sure that Amelia is settled safely into her rooms. The Abbula isn't that far from here. I can run over, put in an appearance, and then come back to be sure the dame is safe.

I only hope Harad is a good hunter and that he brings back a real live and very talkative stool pigeon. I want our stalker to start blabbing and tell us who his boss is. I'm about ready to find Nazar Bettina and put him behind bars for a long time.

The building is just as swank as I remember, and the elevator is stopping at the penthouse, just like before. Now there's his assistant. Marie. A good old American girl. And she's coming toward Amelia with a worried look on her face. Something is definitely wrong.

She's handing Amelia a note, and I can tell by the pasty color of Amelia's face that it isn't good news.

I'd better jump up on the desk and see what's happening.

I see. It's from Mauve. She's looking for Amelia and she says it's urgent—a matter of life and death. And there's a phone number. Okay, Amelia's dialing. I only hope she remembers to check in with Harad and let him know what's happening here.

Chapter Thirteen

Harad felt the vibration of the cell phone against his waist, but he was in no position to answer it. He and one of his men were flat against a wall, listening for the movement of their quarry.

The man who'd been watching them was trapped like a rat. He was in an upstairs room of the abandoned building, and there was no escape for him. It was only a matter of waiting for the two men outside to move into position. Then Harad would step in and capture the spy.

He heard the low whistle that signaled his men were in place. Nodding at the man beside him, they both moved as a team, stepping to the door. Harad kicked the solid wood hard enough to splinter it from the hinges.

The door crashed in, revealing a large, empty room.

Amazed, Harad stepped into the room, his own weapon sweeping from one dark corner to the next. It was impossible, but somehow the spy had escaped.

He looked at the man beside him, who shrugged. Harad walked to the window and looked out. His men saw him and stepped into the street. They signaled that they'd seen nothing.

Harad stepped back to the center of the room. The spy had to be there. He had to be. A man simply didn't vanish.

The loud squeal of tires and a spray of gravel against the building drew Harad back to the window in a rush. He looked out in time to see a dark car slam to a stop in front of the building. Automatic weapon's fire strafed the buildings across the street where his men had taken cover.

As Harad looked on, he saw a dark shadow dart out from the front of the building and dive into the car. In a split second, the tires of the vehicle were boiling on the pavement as it peeled down the road, rear end fishtailing.

"Damn," Harad whispered. He ran down the stairs and out into the street. His men were uninjured and the car was long gone, their quarry in the back seat.

Disgusted, Harad went back to the room where he'd thought the man was trapped. A careful examination of the room showed a trapdoor that gave an agile man access to the roof. The spy had escaped with ease.

From his waist Harad pulled the cell phone that his men had brought him when they arrived and checked the number. It was his office. Although it was late, Marie had agreed to stay with Amelia and keep him informed of all developments. He wondered what could have happened so quickly.

He signaled his men and they gathered in the street

to wait for the car to come and retrieve them. Once inside the limo, Harad called his office.

He knew it was bad when he heard Marie's voice. ''What's wrong?'' he asked.

''Amelia's friend, Mauve, has been trying to get in touch with her for the past couple of days. The hospital has been looking for Amelia. They want to her to come in right away for more tests.''

Harad felt a constriction in his chest. ''How serious is it?''

''They were vague about that,'' Marie said. ''Amelia has spoken with Mauve and she's gone to meet her somewhere. She promised me she'd go to the hospital after that.''

''How long ago?'' Harad asked.

''Not more than fifteen minutes. I called as soon as I knew what was going on.''

''Thanks. Did you happen to keep the number for Mauve?''

''You bet.'' Marie gave him the number.

Harad hung up and dialed immediately. He counted the rings up to ten before he broke the connection. He had a phone number but no address. The smartest thing to do would be to go to the hospital.

While the car sped toward the hospital, he kept calling Mauve's number, alternating with that of the emergency room. No one matching Amelia's description had checked in.

Harad called Marie back. ''Still no word from Amelia?''

''None,'' Marie said. ''What should I do?''

"Wait by the phone. Did Familiar go with Amelia?"

"I'm not certain, but he isn't here now."

It was a slim hope, but one that Harad clung to as he raced through the night.

AMELIA CHECKED the address Mauve had given her. It was a small hotel, rather seedy-looking. She was in a part of the city she'd never visited. The lighting was almost nonexistent. She got out of the cab slowly, paid the driver and stood outside, summoning her courage. Something wasn't right, but she had no choice but to go inside. When she'd spoken to Mauve, the normally cheerful redhead had sounded toneless and...frightened. Amelia was concerned for her. Concerned enough to walk into a hotel that gave her the creeps.

Mauve had insisted that she meet her at this hotel instead of the hospital. Amelia felt short of breath, but she knew it could as easily be anxiety and nerves as any hint of the poison that Mauve said was still in her system. Mauve had been vague about that—something about a delayed reaction. But Amelia felt fine except for her weariness. And that was surely because of the arduous journey across the desert.

She felt something brush her leg and bent down to stroke Familiar. He gave her heart as she straightened up and walked through the front door toward the desk.

The man behind the counter watched her with interest as she approached. "Room 16," she said.

He motioned her toward a dark staircase. ''Second floor, on the left,'' he said in highly accented English.

She felt his gaze on her as she ascended the stairs and entered a shadowy hallway. She stopped in front of a dark door. There were four other rooms off the hallway, all closed. No sound came from any of the rooms.

As she lifted her hand to knock, she felt Familiar's sharp claws lightly dig into her calf. The cat's fur was bristled, as if something threatening was behind the door.

She brought her knuckles down lightly on the wood.

''Come in,'' Mauve's voice requested. She sounded exhausted.

Amelia opened the door slowly and stepped into the dim room. Only one light was on, a lamp beside the bed. Mauve was sitting in a chair by a window that was shuttered. She made no effort to rise.

''Mauve,'' Amelia said, distressed by the woman's seeming exhaustion. ''Are you okay?''

''No,'' Mauve answered, her voice breaking. ''They made me do it, Amelia. I'm sorry.''

Amelia stepped toward Mauve, noticing too late the ropes that bound her to the chair. ''What's going on?''

The words were hardly out of her mouth when she saw movement from the bathroom. A big man stepped out of the doorway and reached to grab her.

''What—'' Amelia stepped back, but the man was quick. He caught her wrist in an iron grasp.

"You've made this very hard for my boss," the man said, "but now you're caught."

Amelia twisted and tugged, but the man held her fast. "Who are you?" she demanded. "What have you done to Mauve?"

"They said they'd kill me if I didn't get you to come here," Mauve said, her voice choking with tears. "They promised they wouldn't hurt you or Beth if you tell them what they want to know."

"Let go!" Amelia was still struggling, but her resistance only seemed to amuse the man.

"Be still," he warned her.

Amelia got one hand loose, and she used her fist to punch the man in the face. She brought her knee up sharply, hoping to cripple him, but he turned and the blow glanced off his thigh.

"Be still," he said, this time as he applied pressure to the wrist he still held.

The pain was surprising, and Amelia gasped. Her knees buckled and she dropped to the floor just as a small black shadow leaped across the room and landed on the man's back.

He let out a startled cry and released Amelia's wrist.

Amelia rolled across the floor toward the door. She scrambled to her feet. Across the room the man was spinning in a circle, swatting at his back where Familiar rode him with all four sets of claws deeply dug into his flesh.

"Get him, Familiar," she cried as she went to

Mauve. She tore at the knots that bound the woman, but they were too securely tied.

"Get out of here," Mauve said. "Run, Amelia. Get help. Get Harad and Omar. They'll know what to do. Just get out of here while you can."

The man fell to the floor in an attempt to crush the cat, but Familiar was quicker. He jumped away and then attacked again, this time on the man's face. His sharp claws tore down both of the man's cheeks, bringing a shriek of pain and anger.

"Go!" Mauve yelled at her. "Get help!"

Amelia didn't want to leave Mauve and the cat, but it was the only real choice. She rushed out the door and ran down the hall to the stairs. There was the sound of someone running in the lobby and she halted. Reinforcements? She couldn't risk it.

At the end of the hall was a window. She ran to it and climbed through. The tile roof was slick, but she managed to scrabble to the corner where a large tree grew. In a moment she was in the branches and shimmying down the trunk to the ground. Once her feet touched, she ran as hard as she could through the back alleys.

Though she didn't have a clue where she was, she kept running. Behind her she heard shouts and curses and the sound of a gun. Another shot followed. She choked back her tears and kept running.

At last she saw a small café where several couples sat at tables beside the street. She ran inside, and though the owner didn't understand English, she managed to tell him that she needed a phone.

Hand shaking, she dialed Harad's number. A very relieved Marie answered the phone.

"You have to get Harad," Amelia said, fighting for breath. "They have Mauve. And Familiar. I think they shot one of them. They tried to take me but I got away."

"Where are you?" Marie asked. "Calm down and tell me where you are. Harad's at the hospital looking for you."

Amelia gave her the name of the café and also the address of the hotel where she'd gone.

"Stay inside. Harad will be there in a few minutes," Marie assured her.

"Tell him to hurry," Amelia said, no longer able to contain the tears that spilled down her cheeks.

HARAD SAT IN Dr. Kaffar Mosheen's small office and listened as the physician explained that additional tests on the poison had revealed another substance, a plant-based poison that took time to invade. The doctor was calmly explaining that they hadn't considered the poison might be laced with something else. Luckily, his interest in the case had led to further testing. But finding Amelia was now a matter of great urgency—if she was going to be helped.

"By now I'm afraid the poison may have become systemic," Mosheen said slowly. "But you must keep hope. If we can get Amelia here and treat her, she will recover."

"She's on her way," Harad said. He checked his watch. She'd left to meet Mauve half an hour ago.

She'd had enough time to find her friend and make it to the hospital. What was keeping her?

"I understand that she has a sister," Mosheen said, looking down at her chart. "I can't say for certain until I discover how far the poison has spread, but it might be necessary to look for a bone marrow donor. Would the sister be a possible candidate?"

"They aren't blood related," Harad said.

"No?" Mosheen frowned. "That isn't good. I had heard her sister was somewhere in this country."

"Yes, but the woman isn't a blood relative. They adopted each other," Harad explained. "What about her parents? Should I notify them to come here?"

"First, let me check Amelia out. It would be a terrible thing to alarm her parents unnecessarily." Dr. Mosheen's pager went off and he stood, signaling that the meeting was over. "I'm sorry, but I have a very sick patient I must attend. I'll have someone bring you some coffee in the waiting room," he offered.

"Thanks." Harad stood. He didn't want coffee, but he also didn't want to refuse the doctor's hospitality. He felt the vibration of his cell phone and felt a wild surge of hope that it was Amelia.

As he stepped into the hallway, he answered his phone.

"Harad, don't ask any questions. Get in the car and go to this address," Marie said.

"I'm at the hospital waiting for Amelia and Mauve. Where are they?"

"No time to explain, just go!" Marie ordered. "I'll explain when you're on your way."

As Harad started down the hallway, Dr. Mosheen's door opened. The doctor came out so fast he almost knocked into Harad. His face was knotted in a frown.

"Is something wrong?" Harad asked him.

"I'll be back with you shortly. Wait in the lobby, please," Mosheen said with authority. He turned and rushed away, disappearing through the swinging double doors that led to the intensive care ward.

Harad made his decision. His car and driver were waiting in the parking lot and he went there, giving the address that Marie had left him. When he was in motion, he called his assistant back.

Marie recounted the events Amelia had told her. "She's frightened," she said. "Shots were fired. Mauve and the cat may be injured or dead. They'll be hunting for Amelia."

THE DRIVE SEEMED to take forever. When they finally pulled up in front of the café, Harad was out of the car before it came to a stop. Amelia was seated at a table in the back corner, a cup of untouched coffee in front of her. When he walked through the door, she stood up so fast her chair tipped over. Then she was running across the room toward him. He caught her in his arms and felt her chest heave with sobs.

"I think they shot Mauve," she said. "Maybe Familiar, too. He saved my life by jumping on that man, and I ran out and left him."

Aware that several people were watching them with open curiosity, Harad assisted Amelia to the car.

"We should go to the hospital," Harad said.

"No! Not until we find out about Mauve."

He held her tightly against him, so relieved that she was still alive. "Dr. Mosheen said there was no time to waste," he said. "I spoke with him. The poison could be systemic. If so, it's only a matter of time before it begins to attack all your major systems. It must be stopped before..." He couldn't bring himself to finish the sentence or the thought.

"I feel fine," Amelia insisted. She eased away from him. "I don't feel sick. Mauve is the one who may be dying or dead. And Familiar."

"Mauve lured you into a trap," Harad reminded her.

"And then she told me to escape and leave her. And Familiar risked his life to help me."

"You're my first concern. I'll call my men to check on Mauve." He held little hope for the woman. Amelia had heard the gunshots. Mauve's usefulness, once she'd lured Amelia into the trap, was over.

"Call your men," Amelia said. "But we're going to storm that fleabag hotel. I'm not going anywhere until I know if Mauve and the cat are alive."

"And if they're dead?" Harad asked.

"I'll do as you say," she answered quietly. "I promise."

Harad called for backup.

"Are you going to call the police?" Amelia asked.

He shook his head. "My men will be more careful. On the off chance that Mauve is still alive, I don't want to jeopardize her."

"Good." Amelia took a deep breath. "Let's get this show on the road."

As the car moved through the streets, Harad caught a flash of Amelia's profile silhouetted against a brightly lighted store. Her jaw was set, her head held high. Looking at her, there was no sign of the time bomb that was coursing through her bloodstream. He could only hope that her stubbornness wouldn't be the death of her.

Chapter Fourteen

Amelia took comfort in the feel of Harad's thigh pressed against hers as the limo idled several blocks from the hotel where she'd almost been captured.

Things had happened so fast that she'd hardly had time to assimilate the fact that poison might be spreading throughout her system. She swallowed and tried to feel what was happening to her body. It was impossible to tell. Except for her feelings for Harad, she was numb.

That was just as well. She didn't have time for illness or worry. Too many other things were at stake.

''My men have arrived,'' Harad told her in a voice that spoke of his concern for her—and his aggravation.

''Give me a gun,'' she said.

Harad didn't argue. He handed over a nine-millimeter semiautomatic. ''Do you know how to use it?''

''Yes.'' She'd taken shooting lessons as part of her self-defense program. As a woman determined to storm the barriers of a man's world, she'd armed herself with every tool available. From weapons training to college degrees in business and history.

"I'll ask you once more, Amelia. Let the driver take you to the hospital. I promise I'll search for Mauve and Familiar, and I won't stop until I find them."

"No." There was more to her refusal than sheer stubbornness or the need to play an active role in finding Mauve and Familiar. She was afraid of going to the hospital. She was terrified of going there and finding out that she would die. At least when she was fighting mere mortals, she had a chance of winning.

Harad must have heard something in her voice. His arms went around her and he pulled her to him in a tight embrace. "I won't let anything happen to you. You have my word. But you have to let me help you. You have to let the doctor find something that will counteract the poison."

"Let's find Mauve. Then I'll go."

Instead of arguing, Harad got out of the car and offered her his hand. Together they darted across the street and into the shadows. Twenty yards ahead, Amelia saw three more men slipping from doorway to doorway toward the hotel. She recognized them as reinforcements when one gave a signal that Harad repeated back.

Harad didn't bother verbalizing his plan of action. As soon as they got to the hotel door, he made a brief hand signal to the men, rushed through and pushed the clerk against the wall. After a brief exchange in a language Amelia didn't understand, Harad used the butt of his gun to knock the man unconscious. "I don't trust this guy. He'll wake up with a headache, but he won't be able to call anyone and tell them we're here," Harad explained.

He led the way upstairs, followed by two of his men, then Amelia and the last man. At the top of the stairs, Amelia signaled to the room on the left as the place Mauve was being held captive. Harad rushed the door, surprised that when he kicked it open, it flew hard against the wall. It hadn't been locked.

Amelia was right behind Harad as they darted inside, and she knew instantly that the room was empty. The ropes that had bound Mauve were on the floor beside the chair, but there was no sign of the woman. Or the cat.

Outside the window, one of the shutters banged against the outside wall. Amelia jumped but quickly composed herself. She stood back as the men gave the room a thorough search.

They were almost finished when one of them called Harad's attention to a stain on the floor beneath the window. There were also dark flecks on the wall.

Amelia bent to examine it. Blood. She pushed open the shutter and looked down into the empty lot. The shutters had been closed when she was last in the room. Someone, or possibly the cat, had been wounded, but had managed to escape through the window.

Amelia took the flashlight one of the men offered and he accompanied her as she went outside to search the ground beneath the window. The only thing they found was another spot of blood.

When she returned to the upstairs room, the men were finishing up.

"They didn't leave anything to go on," Harad said. "What about you? Did you find anything useful outside?"

"More blood." She didn't need to say that she thought the cat was dead. She saw it on Harad's face.

"If they'd killed Mauve, they would have left the body here. We'll operate under the assumption she's still alive. That means we should get out of here fast. If Bettina is smart, he'll have someone watching this place." He put a hand on Amelia's shoulder, a caressing touch. "Now you have to honor your word and go to the hospital."

"Okay." Her last excuse was gone. "What if they call again? With Mauve?"

"You can't help Mauve if you're...so ill you can't talk," Harad reasoned. "The best thing you can do is let Dr. Mosheen take care of you. Once he's neutralized the poison, then we'll do whatever it takes to find Mauve."

"What about Beth?" Amelia asked, shifting her focus off herself. There were other people at risk, too. "You said if Bettina couldn't get to me, he'd go after her."

"I'll send someone to find her and Omar and let them know what's happened here." Harad urged her down the stairs as he talked.

At the street, Amelia balked. She turned and looked

back at the hotel. ''I'd like to find Familiar. You know, give him a decent burial.''

''We won't stop hunting for them,'' Harad assured her. ''While I'm at the hospital with you, my men will be tearing this city apart.'' At the sound of a commotion in the doorway of the hotel, Amelia glanced back. Harad's men had the still-unconscious clerk and were carrying him out of the building.

''He may be able to supply additional details such as a good description of the man with Mauve, that kind of thing. I'm sure my men can make him understand how important it is that he tells us everything he knows.''

Amelia nodded. ''I know you won't give up. Thanks.''

He handed her into the car and got in beside her. Amelia could see the relief on his face as they drove toward the hospital and what she suddenly feared would be her death sentence.

I CAN ONLY HOPE I made the right choice—staying with Mauve. Amelia looked fine when she was running out of here. Poison or no poison, she could have been on the Olympic sprinting team.

Mauve, on the other hand, is a basket case. It's a double-whammy combo of fear and guilt. She thinks they're going to kill her and she feels guilty because she drew Amelia into a nasty situation. Bettina is going to have to pay big-time for all the woe he's caused my friends.

While Mauve has turned so far inward that she's

not paying attention anymore, I'm not real happy with the guy who's holding her hostage. He's pretty much a Bluto character. The last laugh is going to be on him, though. When he discovers I've hitched a ride, he's going to be very disturbed. He thought he killed me when he shot at me darting out the window. Lucky for me he's a bad shot and I'm a quick kitty. Just a flesh wound, though of course I'll play it to the hilt as soon as I get in a position to have some humanoid make a fuss over me.

The car is in motion. I think it was clever of me to have settled onto the back floorboard. There're a couple of black nylon bags here and a windbreaker. Perfect camouflage for a svelte black detective. I blend right in and even though those guys looked right at me, they didn't see me.

Mauve isn't yet aware that I'm with her. I can't trust her not to react with a sound of surprise. Once we reach our destination I'll let her know that the cavalry is still in the vicinity. And here we are. This looks like a neighborhood I've been in. It is! It's close to the road we were on when we came out of the desert. Which makes me wonder if those three riders on the dune weren't there waiting for us so they could force us to change our course and enter Alexandria by this route.

If that's the case, we may be underestimating this Bettina character. Sure, we already know he's loaded with bucks, but he has a real network in place. And he's got the patience of a master strategist. He let us ride through the desert unmolested until he herded us this way. Why? There's a sinister drift to this entire adventure.

The car has parked and it's time for me to get on kitty-alert. This place we're stopping at is a bit nicer than the area we came into town through. Pretty much what we would call upper-middle class—except for the two men with Uzis who just came out to greet us. Not exactly what I'd label Southern hospitality. I'd much prefer some grilled sea bass or even a bowl of cream. To be honest, goat milk sounds good, and that's something I never thought I'd say. It's been nearly eighteen hours since I had my last meal. Kitties are delicate. We like to snack throughout the day, otherwise we gorge and then the results can be very dramatic.

They're pulling Mauve out of the car. She has recovered from her coma of despair. Even though her hands are tied she's giving them what for. I must say that the women I've encountered here in Alexandria are somewhat on the feisty side. Though I'm a male through and through, when it comes to the biped species, it seems that women are the superior gender. Or at least the feistier one.

Enough deep thinking. It's show time! I have to dart out the car door without being seen. The two men are wrestling with Mauve. Now's as good a time as any.

I'm out and slipping under the car. I'm just another dark shadow in a midnight world. They're carrying Mauve inside, and she's still bucking like a bronco. I'm fairly certain their purpose in keeping her is to use her as a hostage or some kind of weapon to get Amelia to do what she's told.

Since I don't know the layout of the house or how easy it would be for me to hide, I'll stay out here a while. By peering in the windows I can get an idea of the inside and where Mauve is being held. Then I'm going to have to figure out a way to let Harad know where I am.

I hope he and Amelia aren't too worried about me. I know there was blood, but it really is just a scratch. Unfortunate, but I have one advantage over James Bond. When he tears his tuxedo, he has to buy a new one. My sleek fur-suit will mend itself.

I've checked out the front windows. The rooms are empty. This must be what passes for the kitchen. There's a table, chairs, a lot of dirty dishes and a cell phone lying on a table. Mauve must be upstairs.

Sometimes the gods are with me. There's a small patio on the back of the house, and above that a balcony. There's what looks like a mustard tree, though I couldn't guarantee it. I like the idea, though. Rather biblical. Even a cat can enjoy a bit of symbolism.

I'm up the tree and on the balcony. I can hear voices, and it's Mauve arguing with one of the men. He wants her to call Harad and get him to come and rescue her. Mauve is refusing. She says that she tricked Amelia once, but she won't do it again. Besides, she says Amelia won't believe her again. Now that's good logic on Mauve's part.

Mauve is asking the man why he's doing this, what does he hope to gain, etcetera. She's a pretty good interrogator, but he isn't answering any of the questions. She's asking about Nazar Bettina. Still, nothing. I hear the door closing. Now I'll chance slipping in through the balcony door and let Mauve know she isn't alone.

Oh, the look of surprise and delight on her face! It's moments like this that make risking my life worth it. I do believe Mauve would pick me up and kiss me if her hands weren't tied to the chair. Well, there's a remedy for that, now that I have a little time.

Then again, maybe not. Someone is coming back up the stairs. It's time for me to do the disappearing act. Dang! I need to get Mauve untied and out of here. I'm more than a little worried about Amelia and what's happening with her. These people are fixing to really make me mad. That's right, fixing. It's a perfectly good Southern expression. And I'm fixing to show them a thing or two about the superior intellect of the feline.

Ye-ow! The kitty gloves are coming off. Instead of throwing a few punches, though, I'm going back downstairs to the kitchen. I'm going to let my paws do the walking—and the punching—on that little cell phone they've foolishly left all alone on the table.

AMELIA SAT in the examining room, wishing Harad was still with her. After a fifteen-minute wait, he'd gone to personally hunt for Dr. Kaffar Mosheen. The good doctor had vanished.

She glanced down at her hands, wondering if poison was tracking through her blood. She didn't feel sick. But that was the danger of this particular poison, according to what Kaffar had told Harad. It infiltrated the entire body before the first effects were felt. By then, it was an all-out war. She checked her watch, hoping that she still had time to launch an attack against the poison. She'd been led to believe that every minute counted, yet she was sitting alone in an examining room, watching the minutes tick away.

Where was Kaffar? And Harad?

She slid to her feet and went to the door. The hospital was modern and operated much as its American counterpart would. There was a nurse at the desk and a waiting room full of people. She went to the desk and asked about Dr. Mosheen.

"I'll page him," the nurse offered and did so. Amelia stood at the desk, watching the hallway. After fifteen minutes, the nurse paged the doctor again. There was still no response.

"Dr. Mosheen is always here," the nurse said, frowning. "I'll have someone check and see if he's in surgery. This is very strange."

It wasn't the poison but a sudden awareness that made Amelia's heart thud in her chest. Had Kaffar Mosheen somehow fallen victim to the same people who were after her? Were they planning on holding him and the help he could give her as a bargaining chip for the information they thought she had? She knew her steps were unsteady as she returned to the small examining room and the leather bag that contained the gun Harad had given her. She didn't feel as safe in the hospital as she thought she should.

HARAD PACED the doctor's office. He'd been sent to wait for Mosheen and he'd managed to do it with a tiny bit of grace—for the first fifteen minutes. Now he wanted the doctor, and he wanted something he thought he'd never have wanted—Kaffar Mosheen's full attention on Amelia. He was more than aware of the doctor's interest in Amelia. He'd recognized that Mosheen's interest was more than medical. With Amelia's life on the line, he had to put his jealousy aside and hope that Mosheen would give Amelia the most personal attention he could manage.

Harad paced the office, checking his watch. It was simply incredible that the doctor was not in the hospital.

He pulled the cell phone from his pocket and called Marie at his office. His men had been unsuccessful in finding Mauve. Two additional men had been dispatched to search the area around the hotel for the cat. Harad believed Familiar would be found dead, but he'd promised Amelia he'd search for the cat's body and have it properly interred. It was the least he could do for a creature who'd so willingly risked his life to help people who were really only strangers.

Harad hung up and paced some more. Finally, he could wait no longer. If Mosheen was in the hospital, he would find him. A sudden fear rose in his mind. Had the doctor also been taken hostage?

If that were the case, Amelia might simply die from lack of medical care. That was unacceptable. Harad walked over to the doctor's desk. Perhaps there was a clue as to Mosheen's whereabouts.

He began going through the doctor's papers, hoping against hope that he would find something that indicated Kaffar Mosheen was perfectly fine and where he might be.

Beneath a pile of papers, Harad found a small tape recorder. It was the type doctors used to dictate charts. He picked it up. It had been left turned on and the batteries were dead. An odd thing.

He found spare batteries in the desk drawer, replaced them and backed the tape up. He was interested only in the last few moments of the tape. Perhaps it would give some clue as to the doctor's whereabouts.

Mosheen's voice was clear, professional, as he dictated orders for a patient's chart. Then there was a pause and Mosheen's voice again, this time alarmed.

''You cannot do this. The patient will die if I'm not here to treat her. I don't know anything about the type of drug you're talking about. My research is in poisons not mind-expanding substances.''

Harad's fist clenched on the machine as Mosheen's voice went on. ''Please, let me treat the woman. If she doesn't receive help she will die. I'm of no use to you.''

There was the sound of a struggle and then the tape ran on without any further sounds.

Harad turned the machine off, picked up his cell phone and called the authorities. He told them who he was and reported that Dr. Kaffar Mosheen had been abducted by a man using the alias Nazar Bettina.

Harad didn't have time to waste. Though he could tell the authorities were skeptical, he gave them the details as he knew them.

The doctor had to be found. Or Amelia would die.

Chapter Fifteen

Getting that cell phone is easier said than done. I just have to get in the house and slip around without being discovered. The problem is there's no furniture downstairs. Everything is a vast open space with no hiding places. The men keep walking back and forth through the rooms as if they have ants in their pants. Why don't they sit down and play poker or drink beer or do the things that strong-arm men always do in movies?

No-o-o-o! They have to be fidgeters. Eleanor worked with this woman one time who couldn't stay at her desk. She kept going in and out of the office, up and down the hall to the bathroom, to get coffee, to tell someone something. Eleanor threatened to nail her feet to the floor. Luckily the woman gave up office work and became a famous tap dancer. She put her fidgets to work. These men are making my job hard for me.

Okay, the coast is clear. I'm in the window—good thing screens aren't used a lot around here. Simple enough to drop to the floor. It's a dash through what might be a living room, if there was a sofa and other furnishings, and on to the kitchen. I have the phone in my mouth, and I'm running back outside with it. Hah! They never knew they were being burgled.

Now I'll use my superior feline brain to call Harad's office. I remember the number. I only wish I knew his cell phone. But Marie will, and she is, after all, a female. She'll figure it out.

She's answering.

"Me-ow!!"

"Familiar? Is that you? Harad thinks you're dead!"

"Me-e-e-ow!"

"Stay on the line. I'll call him on the other phone line and let him know you're okay. He's going to be thrilled."

If the world were filled with Maries, life would be simpler for a feline detective. I've left this line open for a possible trace, if Harad can arrange such a thing. I have no idea what technology is available in Alexandria.

Marie is letting Harad know I'm alive. He'll assume I'm with Mauve and he'll come packing heat with a tribe of men. Thank goodness. I think I see light at the end of the tunnel on this case.

Nazar Bettina will be run to ground.

AMELIA PACED the examining room again as the door finally opened. A nurse carrying a tray stepped into the room. Her face betrayed her anxiety.

"Ms. Corbet, I owe you the sincerest apology. Dr.

Mosheen left an order for us to give you a sedative,'' she said. ''I'm so sorry we didn't find the chart until now. It was quite some time ago he left these orders. He's going to be very angry with me.''

''Where is Dr. Mosheen?'' Amelia asked. She tried not to stare at the nurse, but she couldn't help it. The woman was compelling. She had strong features with dark hair and eyebrows. Though she wasn't classically beautiful, she was striking. And there was an air about her. Not authority, but maybe just self-confidence. Amelia wasn't good on ages, but she thought the woman was in her late thirties.

''I just heard that he's been in emergency surgery,'' the nurse said. ''A terrible accident. Chemicals were spilled and several young children were hurt. Your friend, Mr. Dukhan, is very anxious, but this could not be helped.'' As she talked she prepared the vials and needle on the tray she'd brought in.

''No, certainly not. The children had to be given medical attention.'' Amelia swallowed. Her throat was dry. ''Dr. Mosheen must be highly sought after.''

''I've only been working in the hospital for a few days, but I can tell you Dr. Mosheen lives for his work. His patients are everything to him,'' the nurse said, preparing the medicine. ''In the meantime, Dr. Mosheen was very specific. He wanted you to be sedated as soon as you arrived. He said that the sedative would slow the process of the poison.''

Amelia sat on the table and offered her arm for the injection. ''Then Dr. Mosheen will be here shortly?'' The waiting had taken its toll on her. Whatever was happening in her body, she wanted to find out the truth.

The nurse smiled. ''I'm certain he will. He'll be here before you know it.'' She slipped the needle into Amelia's vein. ''Now, just relax. The most important thing is for you to remain calm. The doctor will be here in a matter of moments.''

The wave of warmth and sleepiness hit Amelia so fast that she was glad the nurse helped her lie back on the table. Along with a deep weariness and an urge to sleep, Amelia felt her troubles slip away. It was almost as if she'd shed her skin, stepping into a place of warmth and light and happiness.

Everything was going to be perfectly fine. All she needed to do was close her eyes and sleep for a little while. When she woke up, things would be back to normal and she'd be with Harad.

The idea of an evening with Harad—without danger or desert chases—was so pleasant she heard herself sigh. His arms were so strong. When he looked into her eyes, his passion was like liquid fire. His gaze was a touch that burned along her skin. Soon, she would be with him. She had to hold on to that.

It felt as if she was moving, and when she opened her eyes, the room seemed to be slipping by her. It was the most peculiar sensation, as if she was moving down a long, empty hallway. Overhead lights seemed to come and go, creating a rippling effect of light and dark. The rhythm of it was lulling. She remembered riding in the car with her parents when they would drive through the shadows of trees and back into the sunlight.

She'd put her head in her mother's lap and the pattern of light and dark would send her straight to sleep.

Sleep. That was the magic she needed. Just a few hours of sleep and she'd wake up refreshed and ready to do whatever was necessary.

Sleep.

She finally gave in completely to the warm pull of the medicine.

HARAD SAT at the doctor's desk for a moment longer, marshaling his thoughts. With Mosheen missing, the only thing he could do would be to begin the search for another medical specialist to help Amelia. Wherever there was one in the world, he'd find him or her.

His cell phone vibrated against his hip and he pulled it out. The caller identification showed that Marie was trying to reach him.

"Hello," he answered.

"This is going to sound very strange, but I got a phone call from Familiar," his assistant said.

"He's alive?" Harad sat forward in the chair. This was good news.

"Apparently. He's on an open line."

"Call the authorities. See if they can trace it," Harad said. "If they can, you need to find out where the call is coming from and make sure my men get there first. It isn't that I don't trust the authorities, it's just that I trust my men more. Tell them to be very careful. This could be a trap. And Mauve is certainly in grave danger if they have her."

"I'll tell them everything. How's Amelia?"

"Dr. Mosheen is mysteriously missing. No one in the hospital can find him, and I've searched from top to bottom. Now I'm back in his office, hoping to find more clues as to where he may be."

Marie's gasp of shock was exactly what he expected. "What are you going to do?" she asked.

"Begin searching for another expert in poisons. Use all the resources we have. If Mosheen can't be found, there's bound to be someone else we can get to help Amelia."

"That I can do," Marie said. "I'll get on it right away."

"Thanks." Harad disconnected from the call.

Behind him, there was the sound of a soft click, then the sound of something dragging over the carpet.

Harad turned to look. A sharp blow caught him above the right ear. He felt his body slam into the desk and he tried to brace himself. Another blow, hard and efficient, sent a bolt of pain through the side of his head.

He felt himself falling into blackness.

THE COLD WAS the first thing Amelia remembered. She tried to curl up into a tight ball, but the surface she was lying on was too narrow. She shivered under the thin sheet, wanting to slip back into the state of unconsciousness that the drug had given her.

The cold, though, wouldn't let up. It kept waking

her, forcing her to think. She had to find some way to get warm, and then she could sink back into sleep.

Very carefully she opened her eyelids, trying to piece together the information that her eyes fed into her brain. Her life had been so strange lately. She'd been in an oasis encampment after being abducted by desert people. Then she'd been bought by Harad—at the thought of him she felt her body warm. He was somewhere nearby. He'd promised that he wouldn't leave her.

From far away she could hear a repetitive sound. She didn't know what it was, but it was annoying. She thought of someone kicking a wall again and again. Some spoiled child throwing a tantrum. She tried to block it out, but the sound brought up other thoughts and feelings.

Something was wrong with her. Something serious, but she couldn't remember what. There was danger all around her. Beth, too, was threatened. Because of a vine with a strange flower on it. Beth had found this plant and someone wanted it.

Amelia struggled to sit up, but her head was too heavy. Her arms didn't obey her orders to push her body up.

There was nothing she could do.

Besides, Harad had promised that everything would be fine. She had to remember his words. Her body relaxed and she began drifting again.

If only she could get warm, she could go back to sleep thinking of him. Just as she was drifting off, she heard the annoying pounding again.

Aggravated, Amelia opened her eyes. For the first time she really tried to focus on what was around her. The room was dark, lit only by an overhead bulb that was dim. It didn't look at all like the hospital room where she'd fallen asleep. She looked around. Where in the heck was she?

The place was alien. She lifted her head for a better view. For a moment the room spun, but she knew it was the drug. Whatever Kaffar Mosheen had ordered for her, it was highly effective. She'd gone under in five seconds.

It took tremendous concentration, but she got her legs down the side of the examining table and finally sat up. The last thing she remembered was being in a room waiting for Kaffar. A nurse had given her an injection. That was it.

So where was she now?

The room was completely unfamiliar. In fact, it bore little resemblance to any hospital room she'd ever been in. It was more like some type of storage space.

How had she gotten there?

Had Kaffar arrived while she was asleep and treated her? Perhaps they'd moved her out of an examining room to make space for someone else.

The pounding was coming from the wall facing her. There was a door there. She listened to the pounding long enough to realize the rhythm was more erratic than she'd thought. Instead of a child, it sounded more like someone trying to call attention to himself.

She eased off the table, giving herself plenty of time to get her feet under her. When she was certain she could walk without falling, she went to the wall. It was cool and thick. There was no way to tell what was happening on the other side.

She made her way to the door, but when she turned the handle, it didn't budge.

Amelia felt foolish. She was so weak she couldn't open a door. She grasped it with both hands and turned with all her might.

Very slowly she let the knob go and stepped back. She looked around again, taking in the room. The first thread of fear laced through her heart.

While she'd been asleep, someone had abducted her. They'd moved her from the hospital and into this room. She was a prisoner.

Which meant that something terrible had happened to Harad. He'd never have let anyone take her. Never. Unless he'd been unable to defend her.

She grasped the knob, and again, twisted with all her might. When it didn't budge, she beat on the door with her fists.

"Help! Help!" she cried. "Let me out of here!"

The pounding on the wall ceased for a moment then resumed with two distinct sounds. After a few seconds of silence, there came another two pounds. The person was signaling her.

She pounded on the door twice, paused, then twice more.

The pattern was repeated back to her. "Mauve?" she called.

There was only silence.

"Mauve?" She yelled the name as she brought her fists against the door again. "Mauve!"

No one responded. Amelia leaned against the door. She wouldn't cry. She refused to give in to her fear. Crying would do no good and being afraid would only cripple her. She had to be strong and think.

The sound of a key in a lock made her step away from the door. She took a deep breath and was ready to bolt through the door when it opened.

She didn't have a chance. A man stepped through, followed by the nurse. The woman no longer wore a white uniform but instead was dressed in jeans and a blouse.

"You're awake," she said, giving Amelia an appraising look. "That will make things much easier."

"Where's Harad?" Amelia demanded.

"He's been...detained." The woman smiled. "If you want him to live, you'll cooperate with us."

"Where's Dr. Mosheen?" Amelia asked.

"The good doctor is indisposed," the woman said. "Now, enough of your questions." She signaled the man. He brought out a notepad and a pen and held them toward Amelia.

"You're going to write a note," the woman said.

The man thrust the paper and pen at Amelia and she took them. "I'm not writing anything until you let me see Harad."

"If you don't write what I tell you, you'll never see him again. At least not alive."

"I don't believe you have him." Amelia spoke the words with all the force she could muster.

"We have him. I fear it was Dukhan who disturbed your sleep with his foolish beating against the wall. Since it worked to our advantage, he won't be punished for it."

"Harad is here?" Amelia asked. "I want to see him." She started toward the door, but the man stepped in front of her, blocking her path.

"You will write," the woman said.

"No."

"If you don't, soon you'll hear the sound of Dukhan being injured. You can avoid that by doing what you're told."

"Let me see him," Amelia said. "Then I'll write what you say."

"If you insist," the woman said, waving her hand as if the entire process made her tired. The man stepped out of Amelia's path and she dropped the pen and paper and bolted through the open door.

Harad was in an empty room, tied on the floor. He'd been using his feet to pound against the wall.

"Harad!" She started toward him, but a firm grip on her shoulder pulled her back.

Though she fought hard, she was dragged into the room where the woman waited. "Now write," she said. She handed Amelia the paper and pen.

"What is it you want me to write?"

"You're going to send a message to Omar Dukhan and your sister. You're going to tell them that they must cooperate with the men who convey this message. They will take the men to the lost City of Con. Once there, they will take the men into the chamber of Con and reveal to them the secret hiding place of the seeds for the orbus plant. Then they will all come to Alexandria with the seeds. There can be no delay.''

''Omar will never do that. Neither will Beth,'' Amelia said.

''Oh, they will, if they want you and Harad to live.''

''Why are you doing this?'' Amelia asked. ''First of all, the plant and seeds were destroyed. Secondly, if there are seeds, they're decades old. They're probably too old to germinate. They're worthless.''

''Don't be naive,'' the woman said, her voice snapping. ''Aleta Dukhan was a woman ruled by ideals, but she was not a complete fool. Neither are her sons. None of them would completely destroy the thing that made their people great. The seeds of the dream plant are worth a vast fortune. I'm certain Omar has made sure the seeds are properly stored.''

She spoke with such conviction that Amelia could only stare at her. ''How can you be so certain?''

''Once Omar is removed as head of the people of Con, I can take my rightful place,'' the woman said. ''Omar drove me from the tribe. I told him I'd return. Now I'll return triumphant, as the ruler. With the plant, Nazar and I will rule not only my people, but we'll control the destiny of Egypt and the entire Middle East.''

Amelia stared into the woman's burning eyes and knew that she was in trouble more serious than she'd ever imagined.

Chapter Sixteen

My little trick with the cell phone was effective. I could hear Marie giving instructions to the authorities. Never doubt that technology has come to the Middle East. For all of the robes and camels, this is a pretty sophisticated place. Soon the authorities will have that open phone line traced and they'll be on the way. That being the case, I have my own work to do. I'd certainly prefer not to be here when the shooting starts.

I've managed to slip into the second-floor room where Mauve is being held. The knots are tough, but I'm finally getting them loose. I want Mauve to be ready to run when Harad and his men arrive.

There's something going on downstairs! I think the cavalry is here, and the last knot is loose. Mauve is free! She's a sweet kid. She's picking me up to make sure I'm not left behind as she heads for the balcony. Smart girl! She's going to climb down the mustard tree. I do believe I can manage this climb better on my own. If Mauve had a set of claws like mine, she could scamper!

We're almost to the ground now. Sure enough, those are Harad's men surrounding the house. Mauve is a little unsure, but she'll follow my lead. Once I make certain the way is clear, we can run.

Okay, here we go! Mauve is right behind me. Another ten yards and we'll be safely behind a building. Hey, we made it. Mauve is crying with relief. Ah, a few little kitty rubs and some sandpaper-tongue kisses on her ankles. There, she's feeling better.

The men are bustling us into the car. It's a good thing, too. Mauve's absence has been discovered. Yes, those are some descriptive Arabic curses I've never heard before. The guards are angry, and now they're pouring out of the house like ants.

No time to stick around. Our driver is on the same wavelength. We're outta here. Is that a siren I hear in the distance? The authorities are on the way. Perfect. We'll make a getaway and the bad guys will be held at bay until the authorities can round them up.

At last, Nazar Bettina's little ring of crime has been broken. I think the tide has finally turned in our favor. Now I have to make this driver understand that I want to go to the hospital.

Surely that's where Harad is. Otherwise he would have been here. But I don't like what his absence may signify. Is Amelia worse?

Put the pedal to the metal, man. I need to see Madame Taurus.

WITH HIS HANDS tied behind his back, Harad couldn't see his watch, but he knew that time was running out for Amelia.

He had no doubts now that Kaffar Mosheen had been taken hostage, along with Amelia and himself. The doctor's unusual absence from the hospital and the tape recording he'd heard were proof of that. Harad could only hope that when he'd been struck in the head and abducted, his kidnappers had left the tape machine on the doctor's desk. He'd alerted the authorities to the existence of the tape. Once they played it, they would realize that Mosheen was a victim of foul play.

Though Harad was concerned for the doctor's well-being, he was more concerned for Amelia. He'd caught only a brief glimpse of her when she'd burst into the room where he was being held, but it was enough to let him know she was still on her feet and still fighting.

But for how much longer?

He'd gone over the doctor's diagnosis and warnings again and again as he'd struggled against the bonds that held him. Mosheen had not been able to give specific details on the poison. He'd urged only expedient action. Was it possible that Amelia was receiving some kind of treatment now? If both Mosheen and Amelia had been taken, it was possible that the doctor was being allowed to treat her.

He held on to that thought and renewed his efforts to free his hands. If he could only get loose he'd be able to attack the next person who came into the room.

There was the sound of conversation coming from

the room where Amelia was being held. Someone was talking with her. Something vaguely familiar about the other woman's voice niggled at his memory. He focused all his attention on listening.

He caught a slight inflection in the voice, the pronunciation of his name. His fists clenched. It was impossible, but he knew that woman's voice. He knew it well!

SOMEONE HAD BROUGHT a chair for Amelia, and she sat in it, the notepad and pen in her hand. They'd given her half an hour to write a note to Omar and Beth. She was in exactly the same position Mauve had been in—to save herself and Harad, she'd have to jeopardize Beth and Omar. It was an impossible situation.

Time was running out, though. She was feeling a little shaky, and she'd seen the woman who'd been her nurse watching her closely. Was she looking for the first symptoms of the poison?

Amelia felt sweat break out on her forehead and there was a dull pounding in her head. Was it nerves or the poison? She didn't know and she didn't have time to waste.

> Dear Beth,
>
> First of all know that I'm fine. So is Harad. We're both being held prisoner by the man using the name Nazar Bettina and a woman who appears to be his partner. They'll let us go if you

give them the seeds of the orbus plant. I hate to ask you to do this, but Harad's life is at stake, and so is mine. They say all you have to do is show them where the seeds are hidden, then bring the seeds to Alexandria and they'll let us go. If not, we'll both—

She wasn't finished when the door opened and the woman came back in. She walked up to Amelia, took the pad and read it.

"So far, so good," she said, handing the pad back. "Now finish with something about how the medical attention you need will be denied to you if there is any delay."

Amelia hesitated, looking up at the woman. "Dr. Mosheen led me to believe I required a specialist. I know you have many talents, but I doubt toxicology is one of them."

"Medical care will be provided for you, once you *finish* the note." There was only iron in the woman's voice.

"I want to see Dr. Mosheen before I write any more. I want to see that he's alive and hasn't been injured."

"Perhaps in your world, what you want is of importance. Here, it isn't. Write or you will regret it."

Amelia's flowing script briefly explained her medical condition and the threat that was being used to make her write. "Then you have Dr. Mosheen as well as Harad?"

''The doctor will do exactly as I tell him,'' the woman said.

''Who are you?'' Amelia asked. She'd studied this woman carefully, and there was something familiar about her. She acted as if she was royalty that demanded the instant fawning obedience of all who came within her path.

''There are several answers to that question. Most importantly, I'm the rightful leader of the descendants of Con. For the history of my people, a woman has always been the leader. Harad and Omar should have stepped aside.''

Amelia knew who she was. ''You're their cousin!'' she said. ''Keya!'' She knew the name from several things Harad and Mauve had said. Keya had betrayed her cousins and her people in an attempt to grab the reins of power.

''My mother and their mother were sisters. Blood is what bound them, but there was no kinship. Aleta was weak. She never saw the potential of the power that came with her role as leader. Her actions almost destroyed the future of my people.'' Keya lifted her chin. ''The title of leader is mine.''

''You want the title but you're willing to *sell* the secrets of your people to get it.'' Amelia felt her headache intensify.

''My people will become fabulously wealthy. Omar has only stood in the way of the future. He's clung to the past for so long that he's unable to see the power within his grasp.''

"He believes the use of that power—if the plant even exists—is wrong."

"I believe it is the destiny of Con's daughters to rule," the woman said. "And the orbus plant still exists. This I know for certain."

"A true ruler puts the care of her people above her own ambitions," Amelia said. Her eyes were beginning to burn and her vision seemed to go blurry for a split second and then clear.

"Tell that to your precious Harad. He abandoned his people to live in the city with the luxuries of cars and fine quarters. Once he acquired an education in Paris, the desert ways weren't good enough for him. He became more European than Arabic."

"That's not true!" Amelia knew defending Harad was senseless, but she couldn't help herself. "He did what he thought was best for his people. Omar was the better leader, so Harad stepped aside."

The woman laughed. "For a businesswoman with the reputation of being tough, you certainly fell for everything Harad told you. You think he's smart. All along you've been wearing the scarab necklace. I sent it to you. Implanted in the gold is a microchip. How do you think we found you in the desert? Abdul, damn his soul, let you slip away. Harad never suspected. He isn't smart. He's selfish, and Omar is worse. You think they keep the secret of the orbus plant to themselves because they're altruistic. It's only because they're men. They *can't* use the orbus and they don't want me to have it."

"What do you mean they can't use the plant?" She

vaguely remembered Harad telling her something like this. Or was it Mauve? Amelia blinked her eyes, trying to focus. The blurriness was getting worse.

"The gift of prophecy is handed down only to women."

"The plant is dangerous. In the wrong hands it could lead to world war," Amelia argued. "Surely you can see that."

"The power of the orbus will be in my hands and mine alone. I believe I can control the use of it. There are no other female descendants of Con, and once your sister returns here..." She abruptly turned away. "Finish your letter. Be quick about it. Time is running out for you. I believe the first symptoms of the poison are reaching you." She walked toward Amelia and touched her forehead with a cool hand. "Yes, the fever has begun. The clock is ticking."

"Even if Beth tried to come, she couldn't get here in time to save me." Amelia had to face the reality of her situation. As it stood now, she'd just be luring Beth into a trap.

"Once the letter is written, Dr. Mosheen will come here to take care of you. It is already arranged."

"I have no reason to trust you."

"No, but you have one very good reason to do as I say. If you don't care to save yourself, you have to think about Harad. If you refuse to do what I say, he'll suffer." She smiled. "That's one thing you can absolutely trust me on. For every delay you cause, he will pay the price."

I'VE SEARCHED the hospital up one side and down the other. Harad and Amelia are nowhere to be found. The Alexandria authorities are all over Kaffar Mosheen's office. He's also gone missing.

Just when I was beginning to think the tide had turned in our favor, I find Nazar Bettina has outwitted me. This is a clever man.

Mauve is looking at me as if I should be able to figure this out. And I should. Someone had to see Amelia taken out of the emergency area.

Wait a minute! If she left, it would almost have to be with hospital personnel. The same would be true of the good doctor. Whoever took them had some official capacity in this hospital.

It's late in the day, but I'll bet with Mauve's help I can get into the personnel files. We just have to find the business office. Let me snag her leg and get her attention. Okay, she's following me now. She's not understanding, but she's following. There's something to be said for a woman who can put her blind trust in a cat. Either she's very smart or very desperate.

Okay, here's the business office. As luck would have it, there's no one there. And the door's locked. Drat. But Mauve understands that I want in there and she has that look of a lightbulb going off. She's bustling down the hallway and I see exactly what she's going after. There's a maintenance man and he's got a belt full of keys. She's batting her eyes, explaining how she left her purse and all her identification in the business office. Here he comes, key at the ready, and she's inside. Now all I have to do is a little slip and slide…and he never noticed me at all.

While Mauve is getting the man to help her hunt for her purse, I'll go through the personnel records. I'll start with the emergency room personnel. This looks like a hopeless task, but the best thing about being me is that I never lose hope. I know I have to work quickly, so I'll start with the most recently hired employees.

I'm sure these records are computerized somewhere, but I'll use the paper ones. I should—Holy Moly! Those dark eyes staring back at me are none other than Keya's! I thought Omar and Harad had turned her over to the police. They must have relented and merely kicked her out of the tribe. Like the bad penny she is, she's turned up again. As a nurse! Wow, that puts a whole new twist on the image of Nurse Ratched. I can't believe anyone would hire that woman as a caregiver. And she's even getting a big salary!

She's only been working here at the hospital for a few days and it says she's been assigned as special assistant to Dr. Kaffar Mosheen for his research.

No wonder she was able to get to Amelia and the doctor. She's been working from the inside. I don't believe in stealing, but I'm taking this file. I'll return it at a later time. Now I've got the file and I'm getting out the door. Mauve saw me and she's already making excuses. Maybe she left her purse at the concession stand. She's thanking the helpful man and mak-

ing good her escape. Now we have to put our heads together and figure out what this means.

HARAD COULDN'T clearly hear the entire exchange between Amelia and her visitor, but he heard enough to generate rage and anxiety. Keya was in there with Amelia. Keya, his first cousin and the woman on whose behalf Omar had begged leniency. Even though Keya had endangered Omar, Beth and her people, Omar had urged Harad not to turn her over to the police. He'd said banishment was punishment enough. Well, he'd been wrong.

And Harad knew he'd been wrong to listen to his brother. Keya should have been turned over to the authorities just like John Gilmore and all the other criminals involved in trying to steal the secrets of Con.

Now Amelia was paying a terrible price, and if he understood the gist of the conversation between Keya and Amelia, there was a plan afoot to bring Beth and Omar to Alexandria.

Harad knew that meant only trouble.

The orbus plant, which had long been the secret of his tribe, was known by too many people now. His mother's worst fears had come true.

Harad had never tried the plant to see if the myths surrounding its properties were accurate. It was said that Con used the plant during the period of her greatest prophecy. She would go to her dream chamber, take the crushed leaves of the plant in a tea, and sleep. Visions would come to her, and she was able to predict future events. It was the specific details of her dreams that allowed several great leaders to change their paths and—perhaps—to reshape history.

To Harad's knowledge, his mother had used the plant only once in her life. The event had been traumatic for her. She'd never revealed the visions that came to her in her dreams, but she'd been terribly upset. It was then that she'd made the decision to destroy the plant.

As Con's descendant, she'd ruled with complete authority. Her orders were law, but Aleta had never led by dictatorship. She'd gathered the people of the tribe together and explained to them the power of the orbus. She said that several families in the tribe had tried to use the plant, but it had not worked on them. Only the direct blood descendants of Con were able to use the drug. Only the females of that line.

She had explained how she feared misuse of the drug. And then she'd told the people that she was going to destroy it.

Only her sister, Rutalla, had resisted. Rutalla and her daughter, Keya. They had been violently opposed to the destruction of the orbus. But Aleta had persisted, and as ruler she'd won.

To Harad's knowledge the plant had been eradicated. Not a single seed had been preserved.

But Harad knew he was not privy to all of Aleta's secrets. Omar had always had his mother's confidence and if she had secrets to reveal, she would have chosen him. If there was any of the plant left, Omar would know about it and he would know where it was hidden.

Keya was power hungry and ruthless, but she was no one's fool. Once she got Omar and Beth in her control and knew the secret of the orbus's existence, Keya would kill all of them. She would do it without blinking an eye.

Chapter Seventeen

Amelia knew she had only one hope of saving her sister and Omar. She picked up the pen again, tapping it against the pad as she spoke to Keya. ''Beth won't believe this comes from me unless I put something in it that will convince her. Something only the two of us would know.''

''And what would that be, your passport number?''

Keya's sarcasm grated on her, but Amelia ignored her. ''When we were little, we had a saying.'' She began to write:

We're blood sisters forever and ever. Blood always tells.

She signed her name and handed it to Keya.

''Cute,'' Keya said, reading it over. ''Now I'd suggest trying to rest. Your skin is flushed. The fever is rising.''

''Where is Dr. Mosheen?'' Amelia asked. Was it her imagination or did she feel more feverish?

''Not far,'' Keya said. ''He'll be here soon.''

"I want to see Harad."

Keya laughed. "He can't help you."

"I don't expect his help. I want to see him."

"Ask the doctor when he arrives. He may decide that you're allowed to have visitors." With the pad and pen in her hand, she left the room.

Amelia heard the click of the lock, and then she heard the murmur of conversation. She couldn't clearly hear everything, but Keya's voice held mocking victory, and Harad's a barely contained fury. She closed her eyes and tried to feel what was happening in her body. Aside from the fever and headache, her eyes were burning.

When there was silence from the adjoining room, she listened for a few moments. Keya was gone. She went to the door that separated her from Harad. Her fingers grazed the wood. What would she give for one more hour with him? If she was going to die, at least she could die beside him.

"Harad?" She pressed her ear against the wood. Somewhere she'd heard wood was a fair conductor of sound.

"Amelia? How are you?"

She smiled at the anxious tone of his voice. "I'm okay. Have they hurt you?"

"No. Don't worry about me. Is the doctor with you?"

"No, but Keya says she has him somewhere nearby. She says he's on his way to take care of me. Don't worry, I'll be fine." She forced strength into her voice. In all of her years as a businesswoman, she'd thought strength and courage were the elements necessary to push through a deal or scoop a client away from another firm. Now she knew it was simply the ability to sound strong when she was terrified, because she needed to protect someone she loved.

"Keya said Omar and Beth will soon be on their way here. She feels victory within her grasp."

"It could take days for them to arrive," Amelia pointed out. "It's funny, you know. I thought that the bad guys were after the pictures Beth sent me. Now I discover it's me they wanted—as a hostage to bring my sister and your brother to heel. She's planned this out quite well."

"Perhaps not. Keya knows the ways of our people. She knows where the lost City of Con is. But she doesn't know the one thing she really wants."

"The location of the hidden orbus plant, if it still exists."

"Exactly. But she believes Omar knows."

"And she's willing to do whatever it takes to get it from him."

"I believe she has all the money and influence that Nazar Bettina can give her. With his backing, she can hire helicopters to locate Omar. My brother and Beth could be here in Alexandria in a matter of hours."

Amelia's fingertips dug into the door. "What does Keya intend to do with Beth?"

"I'm not certain," Harad said.

Amelia could hear the hesitation in his voice. He knew—or suspected—something and he didn't want to alarm her. But she had an ace up her sleeve. The message she'd sent to Beth had contained a lot more than an old childhood saying. It was a warning. Through all of their years together as "sisters," they'd both scoffed at the idea that blood was more important than feelings.

Though the message Amelia had penned was cryptic, she hoped her sister could translate its meaning. Beth was an expert at decoding things. Amelia could only hope she'd find the hidden message in the words she'd sent—that Omar was to be careful of his own bloodline.

"I don't think Omar and Beth will arrive here unsuspecting," Amelia said. She was reluctant to say too much for fear someone was listening to their conversation.

"My brother is not easily fooled, and from the little I was around your sister, I know she's smart. Like you."

Amelia pressed her cheek to the wood. "Are you really okay?"

"My hands and legs are bound. Otherwise, I'm perfectly fine. And you?"

"Unrestrained. I suppose they don't view me as much of a threat. But the door is locked and I can't figure a way out of this. I shouldn't have been so headstrong. I should have listened to you."

"And I should have told you the truth. I tricked you. Tep and Luth intended to bring you to me. I never intended for you to journey into the desert. I'm sorry, Amelia. I only wanted to protect you."

"That's okay. I should have tried harder to understand the danger you tried to warn me about. Now it's too late."

"We will get out of here," Harad said. "You have my word on that, Amelia. And when we do, I'm going to put you on a plane and send you straight to Paris."

Amelia couldn't believe the pain his words caused her. "Paris?" She hadn't even realized how much she'd hoped Harad would ask her to remain in Alexandria with him. Her job, which had been her entire life, now seemed so petty and unfulfilling. Harad had become her world. Yet he wanted her to go away.

"To my favorite hotel there. It's rather small and certainly not a tourist attraction. But the rooms are elegant. The service is incredible. Room service can deliver anything you need. Anything at all. And the bathrooms! I want to run your bathwater and then watch you soak and relax."

Amelia's heart jumped to her chest. "You're coming to Paris with me?"

"Did you think I'd let you go alone? As much trouble as you can get into, I don't think I'll ever be able to let you out of my sight. I'll have to give up my career so I can follow you around and keep you safe."

Amelia pressed her lips to the door. What she wouldn't give for one more kiss. "I love you, Harad," she said.

"Amelia, I never thought I'd say these words to a woman, but I can't imagine the rest of my life without you. We'll get through this and we'll have a terrific future. I make this as a solemn promise. We will be married.''

''I can't think of anything I want more.'' She meant those words with all her heart. She stood up, eager to think of some action she could take. The first wave of nausea struck with a vengeance. It came out of nowhere, but it turned her body clammy with a chill.

''Amelia? Is something wrong?''

It was as if Harad sensed her distress. She fought back the fear. ''We'll have a terrific future,'' she said with conviction. She had to cling to the images of her and Harad laughing in Paris, sipping coffee in a small café in the sun. She would have those things. Keya would not take them from her.

''What's wrong?'' Harad pressed.

''Nothing,'' Amelia lied, hoping it was the only time she'd ever have to lie to the man she loved. ''I'm perfectly fine.''

''Listen! Someone's coming,'' Harad said. ''Move away from the door. We don't want them to know we can talk to each other.''

''Yes,'' Amelia said. She found that she could barely make it to the chair. Her vision was completely blurred and her head throbbed. The nausea had abated, but she knew it would be back. If she'd ever doubted that some poison was flowing through her system, she did no longer. The man who'd attacked her in the Alexandria airport in what seemed another life had planted the seed of something that now threatened her life.

She sank back in the chair and turned to face the door. The lock clicked and the door swung open.

MAUVE IS NO DUMMY. She's pulled the photo of Keya off the personnel file and she's going around the hospital asking people if they know this woman. The one thing she's accomplished is to get everyone on the alert for Keya, who is missing from her shift.

No one seems to know much about the mysterious Keya. She's only worked here a few days, but Mauve has latched on to a nurse who seems to know more than the others. Mauve is handling this perfectly. She's pretending that Keya is her lost aunt that she's been hunting to tell of a small inheritance. Now the nurse is delighted to be helpful. She's giving Mauve an address. It's the place she believes Keya is living, and it's almost next door. It used to be a building that the hospital maintained as housing for nurses, but it was sold and renovated into apartments. Very interesting. Our talkative friend is an amateur historian. And the more she talks, the easier I see it might be for Keya to get both an unconscious Amelia and Kaffar Mosheen out of the hospital and to her pad.

This sounds like the best lead we've got. We have to be careful, though. If anything happens to me or Mauve, I don't know who else would rescue Harad and Amelia.

Mauve is giving me that look. It's show time, boys and girls.

We're out of the hospital and headed toward Keya's. It was a short walk. Interestingly enough, there's a breezeway that connects the building to the hospital. It seems it's been renovated into a solarium, but I'll bet there's a way from the hospital into the apartment building. I'll also bet that's the route Amelia took out of the emergency room.

Little kitty claws into Mauve's leg to stop her from doing anything rash. She's paying attention to me. I want her to remain right here on the walk while I go back inside the hospital and try to find the entrance to the apartment building.

She understands what I'm trying to tell her by dragging her over against the building where she can wait without being seen. She won't stay behind. Okay, so she's going to come with me. It's hard to teach a humanoid to be both obedient and stealthy, but I'm going to have to do it—and fast.

DR. KAFFAR MOSHEEN stepped into the room alone. He took only a moment before he went to the door to Amelia's room and unlocked it.

Harad had pushed himself into a sitting position against the wall. Though he'd viewed Mosheen as a rival for Amelia's attention in the past, he was relieved to see him.

"Thank goodness you're here," Harad said. He nodded toward the door. "Amelia's in there." He looked behind Mosheen for the guard.

"I know where she is," Mosheen said slowly.

Harad looked at the doctor, really examining his face. In it he saw his fate. "Who are you?" he asked.

"Dr. Kaffar Mosheen, specialist in poisons and exotic plants,'' he answered. ''Or you might prefer to call me Nazar Bettina. I believe you've been looking for me.''

He stepped through the doorway, and in a moment returned with Amelia held in his arms. Her head and arms dangled. With great care he placed her in a chair.

''Poor thing, she looks tired,'' Nazar said. ''And I admired her energy so much.''

Harad found he was still stunned by the revelation that Mosheen and Bettina were one and the same. ''I don't care who you are, you still have to help her,'' he said.

''I don't have to do anything,'' Nazar replied, walking around Amelia. ''Her usefulness is over. Just as yours is. To revive her now, just to kill her later, would be rather cruel, don't you think?''

''You really don't want to know what I think. The bottom line, though, is that Amelia isn't involved in this. Give her an antidote to the poison you injected in her and put her on a plane back to America. The people you want are me and my brother, Omar. Let the women go.''

''That's impossible.''

At the sound of Keya's hard voice, Harad turned. His cousin had entered the room soundlessly. She stood with her hands on her hips, defiant.

''You'll have the plant, if it exists, and leadership of the people. What more do you need?'' Harad asked.

''You're forgetting that inheritance of leadership

goes directly down the bloodline. I can't rule until all of your direct bloodline is vanquished."

"You'll have me and Omar. Amelia and Beth have nothing to do with this. They're American citizens."

Keya walked toward her cousin, her dark eyes glittering. "Perhaps your brother didn't bother to tell you about his dream."

At Harad's reaction, Keya stepped even closer. "That's right. His dream. He claims that he destroyed the orbus, yet he dreams of the future. How do you explain that?"

"The orbus wouldn't work on Omar. He's male."

"I can't explain it, but I'll tell you his dream. He saw himself and that other American woman in front of a desert tent. He saw himself as ruler and her beside him as helpmeet. He saw her holding his child in her arms—his *female* child."

Harad understood then. Keya intended to see that both brothers and sisters were destroyed. She wouldn't risk the threat of Omar's daughter coming forward to claim the title of ruler at a later date. By tribal law, Omar's offspring would rule.

"Don't be a fool, Keya. It was only a dream. Omar isn't prophetic. You know that."

"For years he's held it over my head that I had no visionary dreams," she said bitterly. "He must have access to the orbus if he's dreaming. He has it and he's going to give it to me. I'm going to rule. And I'm going to bring our people to the pinnacle of power. We're going to be wealthy by trading on the desire of all other world powers to know the future."

Keya was absolutely mad. The legends and myths surrounding Con had infected her brain and driven her to a point of greed and obsession where there was no reasoning with her.

"If you want to rule so much, Omar and I will arrange it so that the transition goes smoothly. We'll make sure no one objects to you as ruler."

"And how would you do this?" she asked. There was interest in her voice, though she tried to cover it.

There would be opposition to Keya—a lot of it. With her cruel streak and high-handed ways, she'd made enemies in the tribe. Even before Harad had left and turned the care of his people over to Omar, there had been talk that Keya should be banished.

"Omar and I will talk to them. We'll explain the future you offer to them, as opposed to the way we wanted things to go." Harad was watching Nazar Bettina as he talked. The doctor had been strangely silent during the exchange with Keya. "Once they realize the money and power to be made, they'll follow you willingly."

"You're a lying pig. You'd never do that," Keya said, suddenly angry. "This is a trick."

"No trick. You have my word on it. I'll present the future to the people just as you showed it to me." Harad intended to keep his word. While he'd left the desert for the city, he'd spent enough time with his family and people to know them. There were a few who would opt for Keya's vision. There were always a few people who were consumed by greed and ambition. But the majority of the people would hold Keya's desires in contempt.

"And the price you'll extract for this is Beth's and Amelia's lives?" Keya said. She glanced at Nazar, who made no response at all. It was as if he had turned to stone.

"Just the women. You can do what you'd like with me and Omar. Just drug them, put them on a plane and send them away. Once we go into the desert, they could never find us again and no one will believe their wild tales."

He was slowly hooking Keya. He saw interest in her eyes. She knew how hard it would be for her to force herself on the tribe as ruler. There had never been an insurrection among his people. Power had transitioned smoothly from one Con to the next.

"If I agree to do this, you have to give me your word you won't try to escape," Keya said.

The doctor shifted restlessly. "Don't be stupid, Keya. He'll lie to you. As soon as the women are safe, he'll go back on everything he's said."

"My word is my honor," Harad said. "Keya knows that. She's known it since she was a little girl." He looked at his cousin. "Have I ever lied to you?"

"He's playing you like a cheap violin," Nazar said. "Let's finish what we've started." He bent over Amelia, prepared to scoop her into his arms.

"If Beth doesn't see her sister, alive and well, Omar will never tell you about the orbus." Harad knew he had to stall Nazar. "If you want those seeds, and I know that Omar has them, you'd better do something to keep Amelia alive until my brother gets here.''

Nazar held Amelia without moving. ''You're lying. You're trying desperately to save the woman.''

Harad was lying. He didn't know if the orbus seeds existed or not. But Amelia's life rested on his ability to make Nazar believe him.

''Keya is right. Omar had a dream that he and Beth would have a daughter. He told me all about it, and he told me that his daughter would have the gift of Con. She would be a prophetess because she would have access to the orbus.''

He saw the glitter of greed in Keya's eyes, and he also saw Nazar's quick calculation. He put Amelia in the chair and stepped back.

''Get the vial out of my coat pocket,'' he said to Keya.

''Get it yourself,'' Keya responded haughtily. ''I'm not your assistant, Nazar. I'm your partner.''

That was the last tidbit of information Harad needed. He now knew Keya's role—or at least the role she perceived for herself. What she failed to understand was that Nazar Bettina had no intention of sharing the wealth or power with her or anyone else. Once he had the orbus, he would force Keya to use it as he wished. She would be not a partner but a slave to his ambition.

''Keya, please get the medicine,'' Nazar said calmly. ''I must prepare Amelia. If you'd prefer to take care of her, I'll retrieve the vial.''

"Okay," Keya said with a complete lack of grace. "I'll be back."

She'd barely left the room when Harad spoke. "My cousin is insane. Surely you can see that."

"Her mental stability has never been of interest to me," he said. "She has her purpose, though. Never doubt it."

"The orbus may not work on her. My mother was the chosen ruler. Keya is only a cousin."

"My medical studies indicate that Keya is a bloodline descendant. There's no reason it wouldn't work with her as well as your mother. You see, I've researched this thoroughly. And gone to considerable expense, I might add. All of this would have been resolved if Beth had been allowed to find the lost City of Con and discovered the orbus. I would have had the plant in my control. You wouldn't be involved."

The sound of glass breaking was followed by a muffled curse from somewhere outside the room. Nazar reached into his jacket and withdrew a revolver. "Who's there?" he called.

Something scuttled across the floor.

"Keya!" Nazar called out. "What's going on?"

A low moan was the only answer. Harad felt his skin chill and his hopes rise. Someone really was out there.

As if he read Harad's thoughts, Nazar swung the gun back into the room, aiming at Harad. "I should kill both of you," he said. "In fact, I think I will."

Chapter Eighteen

Mauve may not be the best camel rider in the world, but she's one helluva shot with a vase. She hit Keya square in the middle of the forehead. And now the wicked witch of the desert is hog-tied and gagged.

One down and one to go.

We found the passage that connected Keya's apartment with the hospital. And we also found several rooms that have been used for some type of research. Some of it looks like horticultural and the rest medical. If I had to guess, I'd say Dr. Mosheen has been attempting to duplicate the orbus plant for several years. He's in cahoots with Nazar Bettina. Dang! I should have figured this out before now.

I hear Dr. Mosheen's voice, and judging from the fact that he's calling out for Keya, I'd say that verifies my suspicions they're on the same side. Now I'm going in for the direct attack. Mauve will follow up with the artillery. We have several paperweights, some heavy metal containers we borrowed from the hos-

pital and some books. With her arm, she can at least keep the doctor dodging until I can jump on him.

I only hope we're in time to save Amelia!

THE BLACK CAT darted straight into the room, and Harad saw with relief it was enough of a distraction that Nazar shifted the barrel of the gun to the cat. Familiar was too quick for him. He skittered behind a desk.

"It's only a cat," Harad said, mocking Nazar with a laugh. "What's wrong? Losing your nerve?"

"Where's Keya?"

"I told you she was crazy." Harad shifted. "Looks like you're on the edge of a breakdown, too. How long do you think you can maintain the cover of the good doctor?"

"As long as necessary. I am Dr. Mosheen. I've refined that alias for many, many years." He leaned down to Harad's face. "I am beloved by my patients."

Harad saw the black cat slip out from behind the desk and jump up on it. The cat was as silent and stealthy as a panther stalking a sheep.

"So Nazar Bettina will disappear."

"He's already gone," Nazar said. "The authorities have searched high and low for him. He doesn't exist. Only Dr. Kaffar Mosheen resides in this body now. And soon he will be very, very wealthy based on his research."

"You're overly self-confidant," Harad said in a voice so low that Nazar had to bend lower. "My cousin has been detained. I believe you're about to be arrested."

"What?"

It was exactly what Familiar needed. Nazar was low enough that the cat could make a leap.

From the doorway a large stainless-steel container flew across the room and caught Nazar right on the temple. It wasn't heavy enough to do serious harm, but it was a deadly accurate throw and it knocked the doctor off balance enough so that when Familiar leaped on top of him, he went down hard, crying out in pain at the cat's sharp claws.

Using his feet, Harad delivered an effective blow to the doctor's head.

Nazar attempted to rise once, but a red-haired fury ran into the room and clobbered him with a heavy metal tray. He went down hard.

"Mauve!" Harad almost couldn't believe it. "Amelia and I have been worried about you."

"Looks like you were in more danger than me. At least since Familiar rescued me," she added, nodding at the black cat who was licking Amelia's face.

She went to Harad and quickly untied his hands. Together they bent over Amelia and Familiar.

"Nazar said there was medicine. Keya went to get it," Harad said. Amelia was pale, her body limp and unresponsive. Not even the black cat's insistent nudging and licking seemed to register on her.

"Nazar?" Mauve said. "That's Kaffar Mosheen."

"And Nazar Bettina," Harad said. "They're one and the same. But we'll talk about this later. Did Keya have anything in her hand?"

"A syringe. I thought she was going to kill one or both of you with it."

Harad dashed into the hallway where he found his cousin gagged and tied. She'd regained consciousness from the knock on the head Mauve had given her, and her eyes snapped with anger.

Not far from her hand, Harad saw a loaded syringe. He picked up it and then bent to pull the gag from Keya's mouth.

"Is this the antidote?"

Keya laughed. "The woman will die if you expect me to tell you anything. It could be the antidote, or it could be more of the poison. See if Nazar will tell you the truth."

"There isn't time to wait," Harad said, lifting his cousin by the arm and shaking her. "Tell me, Keya, or I swear you'll regret it."

"There's nothing you can do to me," she said. "You've already taken all I dreamed of. If I can take the woman you love, it won't be enough, but it will be better than nothing."

Harad dropped her and walked away. The impulse to kill her was too strong. His concern was Amelia. The law would take care of Keya, and this time no leniency would be considered.

He returned to the room where Mauve had stretched Amelia on the floor. The black cat nestled against her side, his golden-green eyes bright with what looked like worry.

"Is that it?" Mauve asked.

"I don't know. Keya won't say, and neither would

Bettina, if he were conscious. They know they've lost and they only want to hurt me and my brother.''

''I won't go into asking why. What are you going to do?''

Harad held the syringe. He could be saving Amelia's life or he could be killing her. There wasn't time to find another poisons expert or even to test the solution in the syringe. He could only hope that what he held in his hand was the antidote.

He knelt beside Amelia, brushing the backs of his fingers across her cheek. ''You promised to marry me,'' he said. ''I'm holding you to that, Amelia. I know you're stubborn enough to live just to show me that your word is good.''

Her hand lifted to touch his face, and her blue eyes opened. ''Give me the antidote,'' she whispered. ''Quickly.''

''What if it isn't the antidote?'' Harad asked her.

''It is,'' she answered. ''I trust you, Harad. You said you'd keep me safe and you will.'' Her eyes closed and her hand slowly slipped back to the floor.

''Give it to her,'' Mauve said, fighting back tears. ''If you don't, she'll die.''

Harad picked up her arm and in a moment he'd located her vein. It took all of his strength of will to force himself to slip the needle into her vein and push the plunger of the syringe.

THE LIGHT WAS too bright, and Amelia tried to shift her head. It was then she realized someone was holding her and lifting open her eyes.

"What?" She struggled to get away.

"Amelia!"

She recognized Harad's voice, and his touch, as he bent over her and kissed her. "We've been worried half to death."

"I'm okay," she said, forcing her eyes open. "I think." Nothing around her was familiar—except the black cat who sat on the foot of her hospital bed. And Harad.

"Where am I?" she asked.

"Alexandria Hospital. This is Dr. West," Harad introduced a tall man in a white coat. "And there are some people who want to see you waiting outside."

"Where's Bettina?" Amelia asked. "And that awful woman."

"In jail, where they'll be for a long, long time."

"Thank goodness." Amelia felt a wave of relief.

"May I bring in her...friends?" Harad asked the doctor.

"I think it would be fine. You're a lucky young woman," the doctor said to Amelia. "Your husband, Mr. Dukhan, administered the antidote to the poison just in time. We were all greatly concerned for you for the last two hours, but I believe the worst is over."

Harad went to the door and opened it. Beth rushed into the room and pulled Amelia into her arms. "You gave us a scare," she said. Behind her, a tall, fierce man Amelia assumed must be Omar stepped inside, followed by Mauve.

"It was a close call," Omar agreed. "My brother has always been a lucky man. He gave you the injection and it happened it was the antidote.'' He smiled and clapped Harad on the back. ''You always liked a gamble far more than I did.''

Harad shook his head. ''I never want to feel anything like that again. I think I'm giving up my gambling ways.''

Amelia felt her forehead furrow. ''Dr. West, did you say my *husband* administered the antidote?''

The doctor gazed at Harad. ''This gentleman here. He assured me he was your husband. He insisted on remaining at your bedside. Is he not your husband?'' he asked sternly. ''There are rules, you know.''

Amelia smiled. ''Oh, he's my husband all right.'' She leaned down to the foot of the bed and scooped Familiar into her arms. ''And this is my best man.''

Beth laughed and picked up her sister's hand, bending closer to examine the necklace around Amelia's throat. ''Very interesting pendant. I wouldn't have thought you'd find a scarab interesting. Bug of the dead, you know.''

''Very funny, Beth.'' Amelia said tartly.

Harad bent over and unhooked the necklace. ''You're free of Nazar Bettina and of his evil plans.''

''I never want to see that necklace again,'' Amelia said.

Harad picked up her left hand, pretending to study it closely. ''Too bad. I thought I might have the scarab mounted on a ring. An engagement ring.''

''I suggest you do better than that if you want me to say yes,'' Amelia said archly, drawing laughter from everyone in the room.

"Since weddings are in the air, why don't the two of you join us? The full moon of July, Con's moon, is tomorrow. There's plenty of time to expand our wedding plans to include the two of you," Beth said, "Marry in Alexandria and have a second ceremony in the desert." She picked up a strand of her sister's hair. "That was a damn clever note, by the way. As soon as I read it to Omar, he knew that Keya was behind all of this."

"Keya and Nazar Bettina," Amelia said. "Beth, how did you ever hook up with that man to begin with?"

"You know the old saying, 'If it's too good to be true, it probably is.' Well, he called me and said he knew I was interested in finding the lost City of Con. He said he was deeply involved in preserving Egyptian history and also in learning more about a society where women ruled. It was exactly what I wanted to hear. And when he came up with the money—and lots of it—I didn't investigate him like I should have."

Amelia put her arm around her sister. "Look at it this way, sis. If you hadn't involved yourself with Bettina, we wouldn't have met Omar and Harad."

"You're saying it's a trade-off?" Mauve asked. "You're both almost killed, but it's okay because love prevails?"

Beth, Amelia, Omar and Harad began to laugh. Familiar wriggled out of Amelia's arms and went to the foot of the bed. With one agile leap, he was in Mauve's arms.

He licked her on the chin and gave her a little love bite.

"Familiar's saying you need to find the perfect mate and then you'll know it's all worth it," Beth said, barely able to contain her laughter.

"Because it did work out okay, then it is worth it all," Amelia said, picking up Harad's hand and holding it.

"Then we'll have a double wedding," Beth said, barely able to contain her delight.

"Harad hasn't formally asked me," Amelia said, casting her gaze down. "Perhaps he doesn't want me for his bride."

Harad cleared his throat. "I believe it's time for everyone to leave the room now. Amelia has expressed a lack of trust in my intentions. I need some time alone to convince her otherwise."

"How are you going to do that?" Mauve asked with a wicked glint in her eye.

"It's a Bedouin secret," Harad said, pushing them all out the door. "We learned it during a thousand Arabian nights."

OKAY, THE WEDDING PLANS are set and the bad guys are in jail. That's all a kitty can ask. Now I've got to hightail it over to the Abbula Hotel and hope that Eleanor and Peter are still waiting for me.

Thank goodness I have this tiny little scratch from the bullet. It really doesn't amount to a hill of beans, but I'm going to use it to make Eleanor feel sorry for me. That way maybe she won't skin me for going off on another adventure.

I'd love to stay for the wedding, but I don't think that's in the cards. And I promise, if there's any chance that I'd have to ride another horse or camel, then I'd rather walk across the burning sand.

I guess I'll have to think of an appropriate wedding gift to send to the happy couples. Normally I try to match up my resolved cases with a kitty from the animal shelter. But in this case, I believe Harad and Omar have enough cats.

Perhaps something else. I'll have to let Eleanor give me a hand with this.

Speaking of Eleanor, there she is. And she's headed into the restaurant. My timing couldn't be better. I'm absolutely starved and more than ready to get back to the good ole U. S. of A.